# FIVE GO TO SWITZERLAND

Nigel Jarrett is a Welsh writer, a former daily-newspaperman, and a double prizewinner. He won the Rhys Davies award for short fiction and in 2016 the inaugural Templar Shorts award. His first collection of stories, *Funderland*, was published by Parthian and warmly reviewed in the *Independent*, the *Guardian*, and the *Times*; it was also long-listed for the Edge Hill prize. Parthian also published his first poetry collection, *Miners At The Quarry Pool*, described by Patricia McCarthy, editor of *Agenda*, as 'a virtuoso performance'. His second full story collection, *Who Killed Emil Kreisler?*, was published by Cultured Llama, also in 2016; GG Books brought out his first novel, *Slowly Burning*, in the same year. He is a regular contributor to *Jazz Journal*, *Acumen* poetry magazine, the *Wales Arts Review*, and other publications. His work is included in the two-volume anthology of 20th- and 21st-century Welsh short fiction. In 2019, Templar published his story pamphlet, *A Gloucester Trilogy*. He was for many years chief music critic of the *South Wales Argus* daily newspaper.

# FIVE GO TO SWITZERLAND AND OTHER STORIES

## NIGEL JARRETT

Cockatrice Books
Y diawl a'm llaw chwith

First published in 2022 by Cockatrice Books
Editor: Rob Mimpriss
www.cockatrice-books.com
mail@cockatrice-books.com

Thanks are due to the editors of the following magazines, in which most of these stories first appeared: *Connections, The Galway Review, Smoke: A London Peculiar, Mistress Quickly's Bed, The Ghastling, Yellow Mama, The Black Mountain Review, The Ogilvie, Orbis, Fictive Dream, The Lonely Crowd, The Island Review, Tears in the Fence, Platform for Prose, The Lampeter Review, The Cabinet of Heed, Tandem* and *The Ekphrastic Review.*

# CONTENTS

# NO PIC REQUIRED

Meg Lawrence often wondered what precisely her father had been doing when she first began reading newspaper personal ads – the *very* personal ones. He'd just about completed his 'sucker's penance', the writing of bits and pieces under a kind of momentum after giving up full-time journalism. She began reading national newspapers more closely after he had told her in some detail how they had slid irrevocably from grace. He had been a 'name' on the *Daily Mirror* and on the *Guardian* before that, but his three years as editor of a Cumbrian weekly after leaving Fleet Street were dispiriting and eventually an embarrassment. On the morning he flicked a folded tabloid paper into the corner of their settee, muttering 'fucking red tops' under his breath – the boys were playing with Rob in the garden – Meg realised coincidentally that Lonely Hearts columns indeed had become peopled almost overnight by rapacious go-getters exhibiting neither solitariness nor an unassuaged longing for love. These days, all dating and trysts were negotiated on line.

Tommy Lawrence's last days as a staffman were always heading for ignominy's buffers. In the Lakes, his sports reports had immediately caused uproar. A reputation having preceded him, he took to ridiculing poor performance on the field and notoriously lampooned the state of amateur cricket beneath the headline *Archipelago of Dross*, which, as an editor with a minuscule staff, he would probably have written himself. The piece found its way into the *Sunday Times*, and he was interviewed by one of the paper's young sports reporters for a follow-up article. The style and the sentiment had been foreign to his Cumbrian readers; but he had refused to compromise, and there was a flurry of correspondence in the *ST* from all parts of the country supporting his views and even drawing some kind of political parallel. His ire had always been unshakeable. But then he libelled a sports club chairman and his boss had to settle out of court. The following Saturday evening at a village cricket festival, smoking a cheap cigar in the gloaming and estranged from the distant murmur and tinkle of conviviality, he made a mistake with the score and it got into the paper on the following Thursday, uncorrected. At sixty-four, he took his second golden handshake. Without telling anyone, he threw out the typewriter – a Remington screwed to a mahogany base – which he had kept as a relic of a mechanical age. He did nothing ceremoniously: ceremonies were designed to impress others, he always said, and he needed to impress no-one but himself.

Meg supposed that nomads – and her father was nomadic in pursuit of work and shelter – were bound by the likelihood of chance to pass close to where someone of fixed habit gazes uncomprehendingly on their restlessness. She assumed that it was not out of a desire to be closer to her and Rob and the boys that he drove lazily to the South Coast on leaving Cumbria to stay with a friend while he looked for a place of his own; but this particular friend just happened to live twenty miles from them. He once promised never to 'impose' himself on her, his only child, or, by implication, on any life she decided to make for herself with others. He had been as good as his word, yet her mother died warning that this altruism was double-edged and might eventually leave them faced with a perverse martyr as he struggled to stay alive unaided, perhaps a short distance from where they would be able to help him but be prevented by his misplaced stubbornness from doing so. There had been a combative tone in her voice which seemed out of character, perhaps because cancer was battening on her inhibition as well as her flesh. Anyway, he had faith in a home for retired journalists near Minehead and had been paying into its charity for years. At Christmas, the scuffed, *papier-mâché* collecting-box would be brought home and rattled to provoke the largesse of friends and relatives. He would want his money's worth when the time came, if there was a room to spare.

Meg once paraphrased Tolstoy by observing that unhappy families were all alike but every happy family was happy in its own way. Actually, that was negating Tolstoy as well, or, as her father might have put it, 'gainsaying the mighty'. South of the Thames, in Blackheath, she and her mother would wave as he left for work each morning, in the early days on a bicycle, and have no inkling – at least, she didn't then – of this daily confrontation with authority and how seriously he took it. He was forever being praised by people he took to task, which, he once told her, was all the satisfaction to be had from his line of work. What she did divine was his continuing regret that standing sentinel, eternal vigilance 'and all that cock', only made the mighty watch its step; it never, and couldn't, effect its proverbial fall. She believed her mother's happiness lay in a smiling agreement with everything her father did and supported, down to trades union marches and demonstrations: in the early 1960s, pregnant with her, she had sat down with him and two hundred others and chanted on the pavement at the occupants of South Africa House. She remembered his writing that the protests had 'bounced off that obdurate pile'. At home, his anger was confined to the hushed and targeted expletives which interrupted his typing. Apart from rolled-up balls of paper, he never threw anything, not even a tantrum. They were happy – happy and nomadic in their own way.

Tommy Lawrence's arrival in Worthing after the Cumbria rumpus indicated that his wanderings hadn't ceased, even if his days as 'a waged plodder' were now over. He told Rob and Meg that he was 'staying with an old mate' for the time being. They recognised the description as a former colleague whose brilliance had been eclipsed by drink: an apparition of someone vaguely noisy and dishevelled hovered before them, but they couldn't focus on it or even remember where or when they had encountered its solid form. They had always kept in touch with her father, and the boys adored him: he loved to carry them on his shoulders. It was a happiness unsoured by too much proximity. Maybe, she thought, he was walking the shoreline, his jacket slung over his shoulder, his silver hair and ubiquitous tie flying pennant-like at the moment when, not eight miles away, she was snapping a Kit-Kat in Marks and Sparks and eavesdropping on the conversation at the next table. Huddled over a glossy magazine, two girls were reading aloud the personal ads. 'Listen to this,' one of them sniggered. *'Randy brunette, 45, WLTM ding-dong Afro-Caribbean for nights of passion. Photo of endowment essential.'* At first, Meg supposed it was a laughing matter and she smiled herself. Then the puritanical ember her father had bequeathed to her glowed and flickered, and she took umbrage, as much at the girls' stupidity as at the lewdness of the ad. The source of her father's distaste would have been in that part of the Sixties for which he'd had little time: she recalled his saying that freedom was either personal or communal and that advocates of the first were rarely interested in the courage and privations necessary to bring the second into being. He had cited John Lennon and Yoko Ono, real-estate capitalists, and their pathetic mewlings for peace, and she had taken the point. But she guessed he had had his moments. Her mother had thought so, in barely communicable whispers, suggesting, almost by way of excuse, that when you are led around by someone else, however much without demur, there is little scope for misconduct beyond the shadow cast by the leader, the pathfinder, who is himself free to transgress. Anyhow, Meg started reading the personal ads. She even bought magazines in which she knew the boy-looks-for-girl 'smalls' would be outrageous, not to say obscene. So she didn't know what precisely her father was doing when she first took an interest in them, except that the Worthing move was proving to be a mistake. There were reports of fisticuffs and the concentrated enmity of two people in decline, one terminally. The phone rang a few times in the very early hours and a slurred voice seemed about to say something but thought better of it, and the receiver was replaced.

It was towards the end of the Worthing stopover that she saw the ad in the Evening Argus. Her father had once worked on the paper before he was married, so her daily search of its Hatched, Matched and Despatched columns was to discover if a circle had been completed, if the all-time low point to which newspapers were supposed to be plummeting was being reached at a workplace he had only ever recalled with fondness. He would have admired its refusal to be led downmarket. If the stories behind the messages were no longer sad, they were certainly not as whorish as the ones Rob and she were collecting. (The sheen of some of the magazines reminded Rob of pouting, glazed lips). She said nothing about the one that caught her eye: *'Writer, 64, seeks blonde, 40-50, with GSOH for conversation and moveable feasts. NPR. Box 230.'* She didn't know if it was *Writer, 64* that stung her as much as *moveable feasts*, nor did she know why she replied to the ad, suggesting a meeting outside a local Pizza Hut at 7pm one evening. Rob didn't know. She lied about her identity and the white, patent-leather bag she would be carrying, indicating simply that she seemed to fit the bill. The box-number confirmation of the meeting was a brief 'OK', as though reluctance were creeping in. She was deflected momentarily by the dangers of personal ads and began thinking in ridiculous tabloid headlines: Destiny with Rape, Date with Disaster.

Meg's mother once traced the family wanderings on a map. It was after Meg had left home to work and her mother was on her own for the first time, having never worked herself, apart from a few shifts behind the counter of a grocer's in Bradford and some freelance hairdressing at various places of anchorage. Meg had noticed a faint tremor in her mother's hand as she drew the line with a pencil, beginning in Cambridgeshire, looping down to the West Country via Brighton, up to Yorkshire, then across to Manchester and eventually to London, to Fleet Street. She had drawn a musical treble clef, as though signifying the felicity of their travels, never living to see it over-scored by that frantic diagonal to the Lake District or the shameful zig-zag to the South Coast and the house full of empty bottles. Her father wrote nothing after the Cumbrian episode. It suggested to her that it was the first serous mistake he had ever made in print.

She thought he would have been proud of the success of her research, even her subterfuge, if not the reasons for them. She was not sure of those reasons even now. From her parking space a hundred yards away on the other side of the road, she could see the front of Pizza Hut, aglow with its neighbours as the sun set behind her. If what she suspected was true, there was always the chance that they

13

might have confronted each other before 7pm, but in that event he would have had to rummage for more explanations than she, assuming that in her self-created vale of secrecy she was innocent or his moral superior. In the Pizza Hut window, she could see a group of youngsters bobbing up and down in party hats, and an adult taking flash photographs. There was not much activity outside, just the odd passer-by and a few loitering teenagers. Then, at exactly seven o'clock, a man in a leather jacket moved into view with his back to the window. He lit a cigarette and looked to left and right, then over his shoulder into the restaurant. After five minutes, he examined his watch. At a quarter past seven, he stubbed his cigarette underfoot and walked briskly away. Before driving off, she lay back in the seat for a while, watching the tiny partygoers. She was focused on them, giggling at their refusal to eat sitting down, when her view was obscured by a second figure, panting at having possibly arrived late. Then he sighed, like someone whose eleventh-hour habits had finally lost him an assignment after a lifetime of sprinting. He, too, waited about ten minutes, then looked inside at the feast in the corner before disappearing through the door, which closed behind him in almost melodramatic slow motion. 'Let's be having you,' Tommy Lawrence used to cajole on Christmas Day, shaking his coins at everyone. 'Pounds rather than pence.'

# OUR MAN IN BEAUVAIS

In October 1930 my grandfather travelled to northern France to report on the crash of the British airship R101. He'd been to Paris just once before, so spent the last of his four days there, devoting the first three to the disaster near Beauvais and its aftermath. On the third evening, booked into his city lodging in the 18th *arrondissement*, he got into conversation with the owner, who asked him if he liked the work of the sculptor Rodin. On the walls of the small downstairs bar were photographs of Rodin's statues among old lithographic posters and some amateurish oil paintings of the Left Bank.

My grandfather was forty at the time and a freelance journalist. He'd been commissioned by the *Illustrated London News* to cover the accident but had also contributed essays and reviews to the magazine on art, especially of the European modernists, among whom his favourite was Giorgio de Chirico. He had recently written about a de Chirico exhibition for the *Burlington Magazine*, and admired the artist's eerily deserted streets, thinking them prescient. Anyway, my grandfather having divulged his reason for being in the country, and his interest in art, the landlord told him that he might like to know about a neighbour of his called Auguste Neyt, who had been the model for one of

Rodin's early sculptures, the 1877 *Age of Bronze*. At the time, Neyt, a Belgian soldier and telegraphist, had had his photograph taken by Gaudenzio Marconi in order that Rodin could disabuse a sceptical art critic who had suggested that the sculpture might have been made from a life cast.

'How old would Neyt be now?' my grandfather asked.

'Old,' the landlord emphasised, scouring with a tea towel the inside of a glass. '*Très vieux.* He used to come in here now and again; but I haven't seen him for weeks. I think he's still around, though.' (I can recall almost verbatim the way my grandfather told me this story. I'm guessing at precisely what was said, but he was a great one for encouraging the gist, or what he called 'the decorated truth', which also served as his definition of art, but never of reportage, of which he was a stickler for unadorned accuracy. He would have been pleased to know that I was keeping his tale alive.)

The next day, my grandfather asked for directions to Neyt's rooms, thinking he might be able to return home that evening with two stories. He walked there with the images of the airship crash site vivid in his memory. He'd telegraphed a preliminary report and had written up much of a longer account. It was the flimsiness of that mighty dirigible that had shocked him. A few hours into a flight to India via Egypt it had gently nose-dived to the ground and caught fire, killing all but eight of the fifty-six aboard. He'd expected to see smoke-blackened bits and pieces scattered over a huge area like the skeletons of a host of upturned greenhouses, or a dispersal by the wind of some ruined crystal palace; but the effect was of an implosion, concentrated in a small area. On the farthest perimeter, away from the little knot of police, reporters, and official investigators scrubbing the crash site like a buzz of flies around a cow pat, he'd made an astonishing discovery: the charred body of a man, alone in foetal position and unrecognisable.

*

Well, Neyt would have been old but not ancient, my grandfather thought – seventy-five to be precise, and probably still clinging to some vestige of fame by association. Rodin had died thirteen years before at more or less the same age. The photograph was almost as impressive as the sculpture: it was a study of strength and unabashed manhood, the whole effect skewed by an attempt at grace clearly posed to mimic the finished bronze. Despite his compressed musculature, Neyt looked curiously vulnerable, as naked an illustration as one could want of Franco-Prussian cannon fodder.

After climbing three flights of stairs, my grandfather arrived at the apartment and knocked at the door. Inside, he could hear bronchial coughing. There followed an exchange between a man and a woman, the dialogue combative, the woman's voice growing louder as she came forwards and opened the door. It was as though a curtain had been drawn across the threshold, but it was not a drape but the woman's torso. She was bare from the waist up and

17

comprehensively plastered in tattoos, her outstretched left hand holding a flat-iron. My grandfather admitted to me that his French at the time was comically literal. He addressed the human tapestry standing before him:

'Bonjour, Madame. Je suis un écrivain Anglais. Est-ce que je peux être autorisé à parler à Monsieur Neyt?'

But before he'd finished, and looking beyond her, he could see his quarry. Neyt was sitting between a basket of ruffled clothing and an ironing table, near which was a column of pressed garments. The woman said nothing apart from mumbling an introduction to Neyt, tacitly inviting my grandfather in with a rapid jerk of the head. He did describe the conversation he had with Neyt as the woman – 'a stranger to modesty', was how he put it – continued her chore with frequent visits to the fireplace and repeated thwacks as her iron hit the table. Perhaps the two were used to such inquiries.

My grandfather: 'You posed for the great Rodin.'

Neyt: 'Mmm. You have cigarettes?'

My grandfather: 'I'm sorry. I don't smoke.' A pause. 'Did you sit for him often? What was he like? Quel genre de personne etait-il?'

His use of the word sit – asseyez – appeared to confuse Neyt, who probably always stood; that's if he did so more than on that one auspicious occasion.

Neyt called to his companion: 'Zure. Le photographe.'

The woman was well named: Zure. Azure. The tattoos reminded my grandfather of the sea: forms and images floated in a wet and rippling cerulean ocean-sky. She rested

18

the iron, which hissed an objection. From a drawer she retrieved a small sepia photograph. She handed it to my grandfather, standing before him with full, pendulous, decorated breasts, and the first motions of a grin at his discomfiture. At the end of one of her nipples was what he soon realised had been a droplet of milk; when he next looked it had gone.

It was an original print, well-thumbed; perhaps the original given to Neyt by Marconi or Rodin himself, and a smaller version of the landlord's.

As my grandfather looked at the photo, considering his subject to be taller than he, the man himself rose unsteadily to his feet, but not to the height expected. The thump, thump of ironing continued like some attempt at resuscitation. Neyt seemed the epitome of decline, a man bent and struggling for purchase on the relentless slippage of time, silently holding out against further loss – of weight, height, and dignified bearing. In grubby moleskin trousers with braces, and a loose-fitting vest that he once must have stretched to tearing point, he was now round-shouldered and beyond any physical virtue supported by photographic record. The print showed a body taut with almost violent potential, but now only his forearms, as fibrous as tied bundles of sticks, remained unchanged.

*

My grandfather did write a story about Neyt but the publication in which it appeared reduced it by half and published it down page, declining to use Marconi's picture, or a picture of Rodin and the sculpture, or a picture of Neyt he'd taken with his Nagel/Kodak Ranca camera (Neyt's partner refused to pose; she would have been picturesque). The photo of Neyt taken by my grandfather was at the end of a roll of crash site horrors. He told me that the only mark made on the ground by the R101 was a groove ploughed by its front cone on impact. Scrap merchants arrived to claim the metal. He visited the dead, laid out inside a building in two rows, like hospital patients during an epidemic. His discovery – astonishing to him – had been made well away from the crash site. No-one identified the body. Police assumed it to have been an itinerant male, idly crossing the field as something awful and monstrous came lumbering towards him out of the skies after he'd been alerted to its low distant rumbling; he'd caught fire but managed to struggle to where my grandfather stumbled upon his Pompeiian form under a hedge and took a photograph. To that one collateral victim must have been vouchsafed an image of what death would be like, if he'd ever given it any thought.

Towards the end of his life my grandfather was seated and silent. He hated conceits and coincidences, which he associated with sensational journalism. His discoveries of the ageing Auguste Neyt and that burnt body, examples in the wider world of what was coming to the passengers and crew on the airship, what in fact was coming to us all in one form or another, were entirely separate happenings and he kept them separate, even writing about the unnamed drifter as a panel within his main story. Among the pictures on the wall at his home were a framed photograph of Neyt (a copy of the Marconi original), and a reproduction of one of de Chirico's desolate urban landscapes.

As he, too, approached death, brought to frustrating immobility by motor-neurone disease, I couldn't help thinking that de Chirico's cityscape emptiness now reminded him of an opportunity missed: of recognising in chance occurrences and fanciful images a link, a reminder, a nudge, an intimation of mortality, which might offer a sober view of those events and promises in life meant to excite or enthuse us. He left me the small, white-bordered photo he'd taken of Neyt, and I have it in front of me now: it is Neyt slightly out-of-focus, off guard and forgotten, except by the camera's decisive moment, for which its subject summons the hint of a smile. I am the same age as Neyt was in 1930: *très vieux!*

My grandfather was cremated after a humanist funeral service, at which I spoke of his visit to Beauvais and its unintended consequences. The crematorium was packed. I hadn't realised how many in his profession had thought well of him. Soon, it will be time for me to go too, if the predictions are right. I say no more, except that I have known for some while.

# LLANGAMMARCH

Marjorie had done her best to make herself presentable for the court case, not easy for a woman whose cheekbone had been pulverised and twice operated on, leaving her face slightly lop-sided. She'd lost the sight of one eye but the surgeon said it would return: a flickering eyelid would be the sign. Her features were marked not only by the evidence of physical injury but also by the pain that beamed at you from some deep and corrupted core. It was difficult to forget the police photographs: her face was like a panda's with first-degree burns. Such a small woman, such lumbering violence; so much blood and bruising. They said it was a miracle she'd survived. She was dressed in black but not funereally. To the lapel of her jacket was attached a small mink brooch in the shape of a butterfly: a free, fluttering thing yet grounded, and camouflaged as if for protection against its sombre background. So we sought that flicker, a movement, some sign of restoration.

But her house felt a little as though there'd been a funeral. Something had died. Sandwiches had been fanned out and covered with foil; family members had loaned crockery, cutlery, freshly-ironed tablecloths; neighbours had congregated in silence. A faint smell of fish paste hung in the air. Some of us who'd not filed into the public gallery to hear the verdict were waiting at the house and talking again about the only thing we'd discussed for weeks, months; speaking quietly and considerately as if someone had gone forever – 'departed this life', as they say. Maybe Marjorie herself had gone, leaving a fragile shell. A friend who'd embraced her outside the court said she'd detected the tremor of a small terrified creature.

Once she'd returned with her family and close friends to affect the pretence of a new start, those of us in the other room who'd stayed behind had begun talking about Llangammarch, the village birthplace where she'd been brought up. We could see her through the open door, taking the first faltering steps towards normality with smiles, the odd half-giggle at something someone had said. In black she looked like a younger and not much taller version of Edith Piaf. We waved when we caught her attention by holding up a hand and wiggling our fingers, and she responded in the same way. Llangammarch. Someone had just read a newspaper report that said it had changed. These days, it had the highest proportion of senior citizen households in the region, at forty-six per cent of the population. The report had concluded that this was undesirable. 'Deep rural areas', these places were called. They were where the old and ageing sat sentinel, at the tipping-point of a decline co-terminous with their own.

What follows might not be worth a mention, but now we look back it seems to have taken its place on that afternoon of reckoning: 'reckoning' in the sense of speculation yet again and the collecting of stray thoughts, rather than anything entailing vengeance – such a threatening word for those few, restorative hours.

We had spread throughout the ground floor of the house, and the four of us in the lounge were joined by a chap called Ted just before Marjorie's return. Each of us has forgotten exactly what Ted's connection with Marjorie was: a friend of her mother's family, or something like that; someone rural anyway, to judge from the Shirley Temple curls soapsudding over his forehead and the muscular frame straining against what used to be called one's 'Sunday best'. A man in a room full of women, Ted still lived in Llangammarch. It was obvious he worked the land: his hands, huge and scarred and scrubbed to bleeding point, clasped his knees or rested on them through force of gravity, as if in respite from labour. Although wearing a shirt and tie, he'd spoiled his sartorial efforts by pulling on a gaudy tank-top at least one size too small. We couldn't help picturing his struggle in front of a bedroom mirror. If dressing up for an occasion or out of respect had revealed too much undirected effort, his smile was easy and natural – too easy, too natural; simpering even.

Marjorie entered the room at one point to offer more food. We'd had our fill, but Ted's appetite for Victoria sponge appeared insatiable. He held his plate high on his chest and had tucked the serviette under his chin. It looked comical. Around his feet was a circle of crumbs from previous visits to the kitchen. He wore old brown boots, buffed to a conker shine. Marjorie asked if he were bothering us, a joke whose meaning immediately curdled, like so much said innocently at that time.

It's difficult to know how to put this without sounding superior, but – well, we'd got out and got ahead and left the Teds of the world behind. Some kind of travel had been involved, a movement away on so many levels. Aside from pleasantries, he had nothing to contribute to our conversations. When he first entered the room, a mite awkwardly, we were talking about *Le Boucher*, the film by Claude Chabrol that had just come out on DVD. We were all cinemagoers. Ted said it had been years since he'd gone to the pictures, a comment that so fixed him in the past as to find us looking at each other in bewilderment and wondering if we weren't about to appear snobbish. The atmosphere became even more strained, none of us wanting to talk any more about you-know-what. Ted too must have sensed this because as soon as the depopulation report was mentioned, he began recollecting Llangammarch's oldest inhabitant, some retired farmer, whose name sounded familiar, but not before we were startled and brought to our feet by Marjorie's voice raised in anger or distress about something or other. We strained but couldn't see anything either, except a few people converging on her. There were a few audible sobs. Anyway, it was all over quickly, because within minutes we heard her laughing again. She didn't want people fussing over her. As the laughter tailed off, a kettle bubbled to the boil. More tea. Ted picked up his rattling cup and saucer and went to the kitchen for a re-fill. Afterwards, we all agreed that we'd each been been tempted to offer to get it for him ourselves but that the reflex had been suppressed, as if by some firm but invisible hand.

When Ted returned, he continued his tale about that superannuated farmer, a kind of tough rural husbandman like himself who rose at four in the morning and was still working by lamplight eighteen hours later. For some reason, perhaps to impress us or plug the awkward silences, he told us of an incident he'd witnessed as a young boy, when the farmer, almost over-run with rats, began drowning kittens because the cats were supernumerary as well. We were inclined to query this apparently irrational act in a superior kind of way, but waited for an explanation till the end.

Ted told the story with a mixture of bucolic relish and impersonal detail – not deliberately, of course – that cancelled each other out, seemingly leaving us with nothing. We heard how this farmer disappeared one Saturday morning into a barn then came out a few minutes later with six identical kittens, three in each fist. Letting one fistful fall to the ground, he retrieved a small sack and dropped the other three into it. Then he picked up the fallen trio, which was trying to escape in different directions, though not far, because they were new-born and still almost blind. They went into the sack too, one by one, held and hanging by their tails. Into a large zinc bath filled with water he lowered the sack, with one hand closing the neck tight. He dangled it so that it became soaked up to half way. He called Ted to his side and asked him if he could hear the kittens' underwater mewling. It was a joke: there was none. The sack was lifted and shaken out, the six slimy infants falling heavily to the ground as if weighted. The farmer, he destined to see out a parley of prime ministers, smiled at Ted before throwing them on to a heap of rubble, except the last, which he placed in Ted's hand. It must have felt like a wet leather bag, but we weren't given a description, other than being told that it landed with a slap. 'That farmer lived to be a hundred and two'. As if an act of routine culling had guaranteed a long life. We allow him those nine words.

We might also have supplied our own imagined decoration to this story, let alone a moral. For instance, the unfed tabby cat appearing at the barn door with a cry of its own and aching teats, and being shooshed to get on with her job of keeping the vermin down, mice presumably. We assumed the rats were too big for the cats and that there would have been other ways of decimating them, such as the nightly setting of traps. We couldn't be bothered to ask Ted about that after all. Maybe it was inappropriate to question the farmer's behaviour, which it was tempting to do out of sheer mischief. Censure was being resisted in Marjorie's house that afternoon. In fact, as Ted's anecdote ended, one of us had to staunch a giggle: a small dollop of jam and cream had become lodged at the corner of his mouth and a cascade of icing sugar had pitched itself down the front of his pullover like a flurry of snow on the slopes of Carcwm. At that point we each stared at something different in the room, as one does at gatherings clouded in

27

the kind of uncertainty that rendered lengthy exchanges, or even talk itself, inexpedient. As we gazed and wondered, like all-seeing guardians, Ted stood up and ambled to the kitchen – John Wayne walking into the sunset. We all smiled. He didn't come back, so we watched the leatherette seat of his chair regain its shape with a life of its own. Perhaps we were thinking about when to leave and what to say when we did.

Soon, we drifted into the kitchen ourselves. One or two supporters remained there, chatting to each other. They turned towards us and nodded. The rest, including Marjorie, had migrated to the front room. She was sitting on a small settee, squeezed in the middle with two either side. She was that tiny. Turning to acknowledge our arrival, she held out her hand, through gratitude, it seemed, and not fear of being left alone. We took it briefly then she withdrew. We looked around. Ted had gone. We never asked why or where.

It must be twenty-odd years since that Chabrol DVD came out – the film's about corruption of a sort – so we could be forgiven for not remembering precisely how that day broke up. Someone stayed with Marjorie overnight and for the next few days. But we've forgotten when it was she began living a life again. She returned to Llangammarch for a while, reducing its average age by a smidgen. It was where she was born. Perhaps she wanted to set out again from some kind of station reached before things had started to go wrong. She moved away a few years later. But she's never made a mark, as they say, compared with the ones made on her. But that's just us being clever. We had to make sense of it, you see. We think it can be said now, even in Marjorie's hearing, that it had always been a bad match, always.

The cuttings are filed away in an envelope, not pasted into a scrapbook. We all have a set. They are true mementoes. At least one of us had recorded the TV news reports, not that we've ever watched them again; what we still look for is a motion, a further sign of life. It was an onslaught, the judge had said; nothing less than an unrestrained and cowardly bombardment. 'Did you see anything?' we kept asking each other for months afterwards. 'Today. Did you notice a brighter spark, a glint?'

# FIVE GO TO SWITZERLAND

When Karen Thomas flicked a CD at her husband, Frisbee-style, it caused a long thin bruise on his forehead. It was there for three days. The disc was a re-issue of a 1959 LP by the jazz musician Charles Mingus and his sextet that included the tune 'Goodbye, Porkpie Hat', an elegy for a saxophonist called Lester Young.

That's the sort of detail her husband Rick glazed the eyes of non-jazzers with when he wasn't chatting up other women. Not that Karen didn't now and then chat up other men; but Rick always wanted more than chat, as much as he could get away with. Rick wanted the Mingus track played at his funeral and was not to be denied. Sometimes it was jealousy, friends supposed, hence the skimming CD. Karen said he should have ducked. But she admitted that he wasn't around any longer to defend himself against the charge of wanting more from other women than exclusive familiarity.

Seated in the crematorium, she glanced across and noticed among the mourners a large, neatly-bearded character wearing what could have been a look of permanent censure. Maybe it was the seriousness of the occasion. The boys, Benny and Louis, sat beside her and stared straight ahead.

They didn't like jazz; they preferred The Ting Tings on MP3 downloads.

Rick thought 'Goodbye, Porkpie Hat' the most beautiful piece of music he'd ever heard, but its elegiac character had never moved Karen until Norrie Clements inserted the disc, found the track and pressed the button on the crematorium chapel hi-fi, retreating to his pew like someone who'd lit a firework's blue touchpaper and was 'retiring'.

That was the difference between her and Rick: he never needed a context to understand the potency of anything, particularly music; she always did.

Differences. What everyone said about the attraction of opposites never made any sense to her. It was the context, Rick's passing, that had caused the simple tune to make her tearful. She must have heard it scores of times before but had never registered its power to move.

Norrie, their best friend among the unmarried ones, had helped her organise the service, because its unusual content was not restricted to the playing of a four-minute jazz 'classic'. There were things to be said, and readings to be chosen with people to deliver them. Someone read something by Malcolm X, which she thought was a bit OTT and not very Rick, but she hadn't objected. Someone else read the words of the Billie Holiday song, 'Strange Fruit'. She was touched by them almost against her will, though she'd always found Holiday's singing slurred and tired.

When the music ended, Norrie made his way to the pulpit. He'd called it a 'lectern' when he was running through the order of service with Karen and her family. 'Then I go to the lectern,' he'd said. 'And do my stuff.'

Norrie coughed, surveyed the congregation and pulled a sheet of paper from his top pocket. He was soon describing the trip to Montreux.

They'd attended a few concerts, and at a suburban club after the last one there'd been a scene involving some black men and women. The term 'person of colour' wasn't current then. A 'spat', Norrie called it, though even in his bravado version it sounded more serious. Karen began to recollect that Rick had mentioned some incident, but she didn't remember his including what Norrie described as 'a momentary darkening of the clouds' as the audience, such as it was, had begun polarising into black and white. Norrie attempted a bad joke about the blacks having previously been invisible in the shadows. She thought she heard the bearded stranger mutter something. Norrie himself must have regretted the lapse, because he quickly recovered to praise Rick for having been first to intervene in trying to quell the dispute before it became nasty. It already sounded unpleasant. Karen wondered if it had been the reason for Rick's subdued manner on his return from Geneva to Stanstead. He'd been quiet, and complained of 'a cold coming on' but it hadn't amounted to anything.

Outside, leaning against the wall of the chapel, was a huge white wreath in the shape of a saxophone, surrounded by half a dozen smaller bouquets. The wreath was Karen's idea. Rick wasn't a musician; he was a listener, a devotee. A sax, invented for classical purposes but appropriated by

32

jazz, seemed to symbolise the outlandish music, its lawlessness. Rick had died suddenly while listening to an Erroll Garner record. Karen was out and the boys were doing what little boys do about the house. They told her that when Louis had commented on something, his father didn't respond and was 'asleep with his eyes open'.

The all-male jazz crowd, as Karen called them, were in a group of their own, chatting furtively beyond the relatives. It wasn't that she didn't like jazz; just that she wasn't passionate about it. Passion had its slightly manic side. She'd heard jazz fans described as embattled – musicians too. She saw the stranger looking at the floral sax, patiently, as though waiting for it to play something. She went over to him. The boys trotted behind her, positioning themselves at her side.

'I don't think we've met,' she said.

Only then did she guess who he was, because she had often seen his caricature on the envelopes in which Rick's CDs arrived by post. It was the chubby face and pointed beard that clinched it.

His name was Jed Morrison and he used to own a record shop in Walsall. After explaining that, he added, 'Jed – James Edward Donald. Very jazzy.' It was something she was about to say herself. Count, Duke, Earl, Kid, Bud, Chet – and saxophonist Flip Phillips. It was Rick's monosyllabic aristocracy of jazz and its court jesters. She remembered Phillips because it was her maiden name. Once, she'd heard Rick describe Jed Morrison as 'naive' – something to do with the method by which regular customers were allowed to pay for goods only after they'd received them and judged them to be of acceptable quality.

Morrison said he'd heard about Rick's 'passing' from 'one of the others'. She imagined a brotherhood, a conspiracy, with jazz and Rick's other women its secret destinations, the women's spectral presence at the funeral a manifestation of their thwarted desire to be alongside him at the end.

'I organised the trip to Montreux,' Morrison said. 'I do – did – discounted travel. Couldn't make this one, unfortunately. Got reports, though. The pulpit feller seems to have most of the details. Your husband bought lots of stuff from me. We knew each other quite well after a fashion. I'm sorry for you.' He looked at the boys: 'You and yours.' And then: 'Your husband had good taste.'

She assumed he was referring to the choice of music: 'It's a very moving piece.'

'It certainly is. I don't think we can really understand.'

Karen could see the others – friends and family, not the jazz lot – looking her way, wondering who Morrison could be. Maybe some of the jazzers, also buyers of records by mail order, recognised him. No-one else was hovering to speak to him, though. 'Do you know anyone here?' she asked.

He looked around, as if double-checking: 'No, I don't think so. This is foreign territory for me. Maybe some of them bought stuff from the shop, by post. That's finished as well. Jazz seems to be called something else these days.'

'Then why...'

'Why did I come? Let's say there's more to jazz than sales and toe-tapping.'

He smiled and cocked his head to one side, wondering if she was interested in asking him to explain, but all she could do was speculate on how far his naivety extended.

'You're welcome to come to the pub,' she said. Norrie had handed out a blanket invitation from his lectern. 'It's not far.'

With the crematorium marking time before the arrival of the next cortège, they got into the head limo as one of the funeral director's men held the door open for her and the close family mourners. She had neglected them at the funeral as she had grown away from them when the marriage had begun foundering. Their tears and doleful expressions she imagined as reactions to what Morrison had revealed, not to her premature widowhood or her mitigated grief. Norrie, who had organised Rick's close jazzer friends in the fourth car, approached with Morrison in tow like a spare part at a wedding, as Rick was fond of saying, though more indelicately. Both stopped short when she held her hand to the window, palm outwards. All right, OK, you win, they seemed to be saying, backing off then fixed to the spot as the limo's engine murmured into life. But not really, nothing so harsh. The words were from a tune made famous by – who was it now? – Joe someone, Joe Williams. Yes, Joe Williams. She looked at the boys, who had had death explained to them to their infantile satisfaction. They were already plugged in, listening to someone or other. Someone else. And quietly she began to hum a tune of her own. Later, after everyone had spoken to her and the boys were outside in the beer garden being looked after by Norrie or the relatives, Morrison approached her again when she was briefly on her own. 'Can I get you anything?' he asked. She smiled and shook her head.

They said nothing for a few minutes, imagining grief to be biding its time. Then Morrison placed his glass on the table and re-arranged himself in his seat.

'That trip to Montreux,' he said. 'Do you know anything about it?'

After staring into space, she turned her face towards him slowly and blinked, like someone on medication. His question sounded to her as if he were seeking more facts.

'No,' she said. 'I'm afraid I can't help you.'

He chuckled. 'No, I didn't mean that. The fellow in the pulpit didn't say all that much.'

Karen was interested now. 'Go on,' she said.

'Well, you know what tours are like, trips abroad, all male.'

She looked at him quizzically, her brow furrowed at more of his innocence. 'Actually, no, I don't.'

Morrison then embarked inexplicably on a long screed which Karen would afterwards liken to a fifteen-minute solo by another saxophonist, John Coltrane, but without its 'ugliness and its dismal lack of interest'. Rick had once handed her a book on jazz by the poet Philip Larkin, who had criticised Coltrane for 'being ugly on purpose'.

'Your husband deserved a medal after that Swiss business,' Morrison said. 'As I heard it, there were three of them at the bar, including your husband and the Norrie fellow. The other two on the trip were sitting at a table, listening to the band. It was a blues singer and two electric guitars plus drums. Pretty deafening, I should think. There were three women at the bar with the men, having drinks. Black women. I mention their colour because it's relevant. Five visiting white men, three coloured women, and a few locals. That's jazz for you.'

He waited for her to laugh but she was just staring at him, almost through him. She was waiting for him to continue, curious as to why he was telling her all this.

'A couple of other black guys come into the club,' he said. 'They see the six at the bar and walk towards them, bumping into the table with the two other friends of your husband and knocking over a drink. They look mean. One of the seated friends tells the new black guys to watch where they're going. One of the black guys turns around and picks your husband's friend up by the lapels. The other friend pushes him away. The other black guy wades in.

' Your husband's two friends at the bar, the drinkers, go to sort things out. The band stops playing and the drummer steps forward and clouts one of your husband's drinking friends. By now the black women are screaming. Your husband's two drinking pals try to do something but get clobbered. One of the newcomers pulls a knife. Your husband goes forward. The black woman he's with tries to hold him back but fails. Your husband tries to talk to the guy with the knife. Someone hits him from behind. The knife guy takes a threatening lunge at someone, your husband reaches up and grabs his wrist. Then it all gets confused. Someone steps in, maybe some new punters turning up – that's what I was told. Anyway, it quietened down and the band started playing again. No-one got really hurt. The two troublesome black guys left with two of the drinking women. He tried to grab the knife, did your husband. Very brave.'

He reached in his wallet for a Polaroid-type photo and handed it to her. It showed Rick and Norrie at the bar with one of the women between them, her arms around their shoulders. It must have been taken before things turned unsavoury. They're all smiles. Karen found the woman's ebony beauty alluring beyond any standard from which other women, women like her at home with two kids, would regularly fall. Before the attentions of such a woman, men were defenceless. That woman – dark, glistening, voluptuous – looked as though she could deal with men two at a time. She was not a rival but an idol, Karen thought. The word 'idol' amused her. But she knew what she meant. She also knew at last the extent of Morrison's lack of guile.

'Where did you get this?' she asked.

'Oh, I had to pop across and sort something out, something unrelated. I went over there a lot – the Continent. I found the club. Your husband told me about it, about what happened.'

'Your story was from him?'

'Yes, partly. And from some chap behind the bar who saw it all. He pointed to the picture – it was pinned up with others above the bar. He let me have it. There's a picture of Charlie Mariano up there too – and Palle Mikkelborg.'

She found these names vaguely familiar but unimpressive and they slipped past her with a lot of other things, an ever-accelerating procession of bad experiences. She handed back the picture and shook her head when Morrison asked if she wanted to keep it.

They must have been standing there for a while, waiting for Morrison to finish his story – Norrie, with Benny and Louis at his side, each holding his hand, like orphans who'd discovered a substitute father. She asked Norrie: 'What happened to your woman, then?' with the emphasis on the 'your'. Norrie, mystified, looked to Morrison for some clue.

But without waiting for an answer and leaving the two men stranded, she called the boys forward. The family members were gathering. 'Come along, you guys,' she said. 'It's time we were making a move.'

# A FRIEND OF JOE ORTON

Rick it was who first spotted the headless kid floating off the pier. Things went something like this: saw torso, phoned police, gave statement, went to the Dancers and told Basil Cutts because he was the first in.

Basil used to live by Rick in Lealand Road, it turned out, but he didn't know until as a teenager he was in that play at the youth club and Basil came down to advise them. Struck a lot of unhelpful poses did Basil, nothing to do with the production, which was about teenage pregnancy. Buns in the baby Belling, some wag commented.

Now, Basil was in a basement flat in Arundel Square, visited each day by Mrs Chandranarth, emissary from Islington social services. She called him 'Sir' Basil. Basil said he could trump the torso 'cos he'd seen the room where Ken Halliwell had whacked the playright Joe Orton to death with a claw hammer. It was the 'claw' bit that did it for many. Rick wanted to be an actor, *was* an actor. 'Ak-taw,' his father smirked behind the crinkling *Morning Star*. But not like Basil. They said Basil couldn't get parts any more because his memory was going. Someone else said Mrs Chandranarth was sticking labels on everything in the flat – kettle, table, vase, tea-strainer. Had a peel-off roll of them. Basil had been seen and/or heard one night ranting at the noise coming from the Daughters of Niger Apostolic Church. Rick wanted to impress Basil but the nipper's corpse couldn't do it. 'Ritual killing,' Basil told him, as if they were thirteen to the dozen down Woolwich Reach. 'That room was a mess. Brains everywhere.'

Rick had just 'walked' in EastEnders. It was Equity stuff. You had to keep out the huggers. He'd also been in a two-hander at the Regent. Not a bad piece, about a carer (played by Rick) and an ageing stand-up in a nursing home who was making the old girls piss their drawers with selections from his blue book. Liability. Anyway, Rick had gone back to the club on the strength of his Albert Square dawdle (actually he was in shot for fifteen seconds, leather-jacketed, chatting to someone, but you couldn't hear anything) and a few other board bobs. It had all changed down there with the airports. Said floater still had its trainers on, feet like upturned twin rudders. Must have been waltzing up and down for a while, the police said. On the tide, snagged for most of the time among the timbers, bumping into them silently like a pinball. Rick had got back to the Dancers at about eight. Basil was telling Hils the bartender Coward's St Dunstan's joke, possibly for the thirty-first time: 'Two dogs *in flagrante delicto* appear at a bend in the path,' he said. 'Coward minor asks nurse what's afoot. Nurse says the canine in front is blind and the one behind is pushing it to St Dunstan's.' A smile from glass-wiping Hils, a wink in Rick's direction. Bulging walls, smoke, mild carbolic, signed photos of dead celebs on a slant – Joe Loss, Erik Chitty, Beryl Reid, Peter Cavanagh. Eight was early. No-one arrived without an audience if they could help it. You were talking nine-fifteen at least. Time for the Orton thing. Basil knew Coward, balding Brylcreemed smoker with pendulous silk scarf, head round dressing-room door. Or so he said. It sounded like the description you could mug from a publicity still.

'Did you know that Halliwell's mother was stung by a wasp and choked to death in front of him, when he was still a nipper?' Basil asked.

Rick didn't. Hils was listening in, leaning on the bar, hands in prayer mode, teacloth over his shoulder. But no smile. Rick wondered if Basil expected them to consider this trauma a reason for the later cranium-crunching and suicide: Rick knew that Halliwell, straight after the deed, popped so many Nembies he must have been cuckoo before he'd finished the bottle. Found half-naked. covered in blood. Orton's skull, it was said, resembled the crater of an extinguished candle. No more acerbic wit from him, or last-in-the-heats stuff from his boyfriend.

If Mrs Chandranarth's diagnosis was pure Caribbean schmink, there was definitely something up with Basil. Like in the way he went off down byways, leading you through a maze. So nothing more about friend Halliwell, not directly anyway.

'*Entertaining Mr Sloane*'s a great play, but old man Kemp has no spirit left, no fight,' he said. 'Little wonder Mr Sloane goes for him – literally. Mr Sloane re-awakens old sexual feelings in Kath and Ed, they even see possibilities, but old Kemp knows only that his boss was murdered by Mr Sloane

42

and that his boss was a sleazy photographer. The *Ham 'n' High's* critic said I made old Kemp seem years younger. It was rage that did it. The light is dead in Kemp. For him, Sloane just casts shadows. I saw him a few times here – Orton, I mean. With his boyfriend. Full of himself. The boy friend said nothing, of course, just scowled.'

Hils pitched in, sensing Rick's exasperation: 'So this play, was it prophetic?'

Basil looked across at Hils, as though the barman was one of those ditch-diggers who can surprise you with a quote from Voltaire. He stared for a while, not contemptuously any more but as someone whose brain is re-navigating its position. It honed in again on mayhem and wild theatrical apocrypha.

'August the 8th 1967 is a date engraven on my memory,' he intones, as if quoting a line from a play. 'I'd been promised a part in *Up Against It*, you see. Not the stage thing – that poof Brian Epstein didn't want it. But the film. Oscar Lewenstein. I knew Joe, even knew where the front door key was hidden for that Noel Road flat. Anyway, I went in, thought I'd get Joe to put in a word for me. Joe was as brown as a berry. Halliwell, too. I could see him hammering something into the kitchen wall, a picture hook or something. Joe had a graze on his cheek, with a bruise forming. He didn't get that crashing a kiddy car, I can tell you. We chatted some. No part, though. Peggy Ramsey rang me next day to say the two were dead. The police interviewed me. I mentioned the cheek. Rang a couple of newspapers and *The Stage* with my story. What fucking story? they all said. They didn't say fucking. I thought I was the last to see them. I wasn't, it turned out. Halliwell died first. Did you know? No talent for murder, either.'

Rick got all the bumf on Orton and Halliwell that time he was in *Ruffian on the Stair* at the King's Head. By that time Basil was dead, too. Found in his flat by Mrs Chandranarth, bending over to look through the letterbox like a fat seaside landlady in a Bamforth postcard. Had Basil made that August 8th story up? Nobody knew. Rick hadn't got to know him well enough. All he remembers vividly, anecdotally, now is catching up with him in Farringdon Street on the way to the Dancers one blustery night. Sir Basil, in green Robin Hood hat, camel-hair coat, half-mast cavalry twills and dirty suede shoes was fighting with an inverted umbrella. It was a defeat. 'Dead and never called me mother,' he said to Rick as they headed into the rain. It was dark, and coming up to 9.15pm.

It was a ritual killing, apparently, to do with one of the ethnic communities and some bizarre cult within that. It still preys on Rick's mind. He swears the Basil stuff is true. Rick says Hils said Basil was great entertainment value. Which, for an entertainer, is not bad schtick. Mrs Chandranarth's case-load was reduced by one then increased by six. Walking down from Caledonian Road tube one Saturday evening, Rick began picking up the Daughters of Niger Church choristers at three hundred paces. In London, there was much to take one's mind off things.

# LOVEY-DOVEY

When Kate's mobile rumbled into life on her bedside table, it briefly entered her dreams as a burping frog that someone was daring her to pick up. She looked at the time: it was ten past three in the morning. The number wasn't one she recognised.

'Hello,' she half-whispered, as if there were someone else in the room who was not to be disturbed. There was no-one. There hadn't been for a while now.

'Lorna?'

It was a man's voice.

'No. This is Kate. Kate Griffiths. Who's this?'

'Katie?' A pause. 'Oh my god!'

It was a long while since she'd heard him speak – almost two years – but she knew who it was.

'Guy?'

'Yes, Oh, this is awful. I'm so sorry, Kate. I'll let you get back to bed. Were you in bed? Were you asleep? Did I wake you?'

'Wait. Why are you ringing anyone at this hour of the night?'

'It's not night; it's morning.'

She sat up and smiled. That was Guy Morris all over: full of questions and pointlessly precise. Infuriating. She put the light on.

'So – what's up?'

There was a sigh at the other end of the line, the prelude to a gathering of his thoughts, or annoyance at his stupidity. No, the first.

'It's about Mike,' he explained 'Mike Johnson. You remember Mike.'

It was Mike, or an amalgam of Mike and others, who appearing as a child she could not possibly have known had dared her to close her fingers around that slimy amphibian. No, not Mike; if there, he would have stood back, to observe the others with a certain amount of disinclination and distaste. Frogs were not slimy or wet, anyway. She'd learned that, like a lot of other things. But the dream was already fading.

'Yes.' She said it in a way that meant 'Of course'.

'He's... oh, look. I'm sorry. I should go. I'll get in touch and tell you everything. Bye.'

And he rang off.

Still clutching the phone, she swung out of bed and walked to the window. The street was deserted, an orange-neon expanse, except that trotting down the pavement on the opposite side of the road was a fox. The lurid lights made it look grey, wolf-like. It reached a skip parked outside the flats across the way, rose on its hind legs and began to paw at the overhanging rubbish. She aimed the phone to take a picture but, as it clicked and flashed, the fox dropped on all fours and continued on its way. She didn't delete the picture, an abstract smudge. She rarely deleted anything. Deep in the phone's cavernous memory there was probably still a picture of Guy. And Mike. All of them together in happier times. No, not happier times: careless times. A combined selfie. She remembered Lorna as someone pretty who briefly flickered moth-like into their circle. Perhaps Lorna was next to Kate in his contacts list and he'd dialled in error. But that would mean she, Kate Griffiths, was still in the scroll.

With Guy things had become serious. The two of them used to laugh at that expression, as if love, or whatever it was, no longer had room for jokes and levity but was ever ready to cope with bad news, with tragedy. Perhaps 'tragedy' was too strong a word and 'serious' was OK, meaning both were prepared to put themselves out for the other. They just hoped that personal misfortune would pass them by. Why wouldn't it? Awful things were bound to happen, but they'd be ready for them. One Christmas, he'd sneaked from an album the head-and-shoulders photo she'd had taken at school when she was eight, and had it framed alongside his, taken at the same age but in a different place. She'd kept the double portrait until they broke up, when she tapped it gently, retrieved the pictures and thrown away the glass shards and the frame. She'd returned his picture to him but he didn't reply. She wished she hadn't. She wondered if he'd received it. Mike Johnson, though – he was an intense, brooding sort of chap, a so-called 'silent type', unluckier in love than even she was, and more likely

47

than Guy to have thought of that twin portrait idea. Perhaps he had.

In work several hours later, she couldn't concentrate on anything except Guy's call. There'd been no reason why they couldn't have remained friends, but it never happened. She'd had little contact with Mike, and she wondered what was up. Memories began leaking back: of Mike, for instance, always vaguely seeking something.

A couple of days went by without a follow-up call. She delved into her Gallery. No Guy. There was one of Mike, in the rear and gloomily half-grinning with her and a couple of friends on a night out. Perhaps she'd got rid of Guy's after all, in a furious aftermath that had lost its detail – the woman scorned by men, all men. She'd done a lot in anger at that time, a lot she'd forgotten about.

She couldn't have made a fresh start without ridding herself of the bitterness, the memories that had turned bad. It had been like weeding a garden, she remembered, a small corrupted plot.

On the third day she found herself staring at Guy's number in her phone log. She didn't think it was the one he had when they were together. That he hadn't rung again, as promised, posed a dilemma. Did it mean she and the early morning call had slipped his memory? And would a pre-emptive approach by her be the sort of thing he might expect, and begin making the assumptions she was determined to avoid? She gave him the benefit of the doubt after work, and rang his number.

'Kate! How nice to hear from you,' he said. She could hear him zapping down the volume of the TV. She added no more, but waited for him to continue, to explain himself. 'Sorry again about the other night – er, morning. I didn't know what I was doing. Been in a bit of a fog with this and that.'

'So what's up with Mike?' She wasn't in the mood for banter. She couldn't imagine Guy being 'in a fog' about anything, except being spurned by a woman.

'Well, he just turned up here an hour before I got through to you by mistake. Lorna had ditched him. He didn't know why. Frankly, he was in a state, wanted to stay the night. Bloody suicidal, if you can believe it. You know Mike: head over heels in love but always with someone not half as barmy. He'd been walking the streets. I heard him out – it was all to do with Lorna not being what he called 'responsive' – and got him a taxi. I tried to ring Lorna after I spoke to you; sorry again! I was worried about her because he said he'd chucked something at her and split her lip. Maybe that was a while ago. I was also worried about him, but not to the extent of wanting him to sleep on my settee, though I offered. I couldn't get through. It's great to hear your voice again, really.'

'Have you spoken to Lorna since? I hardly know her.'

'Nor did I until we were introduced. I got in touch the next day, or several hours later. She said Mike was too intense. Did you know he sent her flowers every two weeks, on the dot? Well, no, you wouldn't. But he did. Very lovey-dovey. Never says much, then goes doolally romantic.'

She didn't want to sound as though she'd made more than a courtesy call, a curiosity call: 'Is that it?'

'More or less. He'll get over it.'

Another pause.

'How are you, Guy?

'I'm surviving. And you?'

'Fine. Everything's good.'

'You should have a word with Mike.'

'What!'

'I mean, you might be able to help. I'm useless. You know what we men are like; not the amorous types. You were always the sensible one. He'd love to talk to you. I'm surprised you haven't kept in touch with the old crowd.'

'Perhaps I have. Anyway, now you've bloody well got my number. I should have thought of that.'

Actually, she hadn't seen many of them. They weren't a crowd any more. She'd split with Guy because he never understood the important issues, didn't even see them as a problem. He had no right to say she was sensible; she wasn't. Now that Guy had done some mild raking over that corrupted, weeded plot, Mike Johnson came into sharper focus. She recalled birthday parties, hen nights (at which Mike had been mentioned, though not discussed), trips to the theatre, weddings, christenings. At least a few of them were always present, like those dolls that spring upright however much you try to push them over. Next thing she heard, from afar a year ago, Lorna and Mike were together. Mike was good-looking and gallant – chivalrous – in a sweet sort of way. Others had got married and moved off to new lives, new friends, new interests. It wasn't anyone sensible Mike needed now; it was someone who felt the same way as he did. Sensible didn't necessarily mean tender-hearted. Did she square up? Perhaps she did. So he threw things, he could get angry. She grinned. Well, it was better than being uncaring and sullen – and befogged.

That night, she couldn't sleep. At two o'clock she got up and looked out of the window. The skip was still there, piled even higher with objects unwanted and jettisoned. Nothing stirred. Did the fox follow the same trail every time? She stood there, waiting for it to appear, and the uncommonly quiet city, windless, straight away took on an air of expectancy. Was it a dog fox or a vixen she'd seen after Guy had rung? Were there cubs, being looked after by the mate? She'd read about urban foxes, and watched a TV documentary about them. It was as if a new environment had been foisted on them, rather than that they'd entered it of their own accord. Either way, it seemed a dangerous life for a fox, and she thought of the trotting one – yes, trotting – she'd seen before, keen, courting danger, but alive – a true survivor, not like Guy, who said he was surviving probably in order to emphasise a loss still being felt, something missing; namely a woman, she as good as anyone else. No way, as Guy used to say in lieu of debating anything. Why would Mike throw things? Was he short-tempered or exasperated? Not many rows with Guy ended in frenzied love-making. They should, she thought. She'd just finished reading *The Smoking Diaries* by Simon Gray, all four volumes in one brick-size book. The dispersed gang loved the theatre; well, they went fairly often. While smoking in an act of complicity, she'd noted some things, wise or inscrutable, the author had written. Death, he said, was 'a great and romantic adventure'. One of that dreamtime amalgam, watching her as she reached down to touch the frog, was heard to comment, 'Ugh...I'd rather die than do that.' She hadn't touched it or picked it up.

She didn't ask Guy for Mike's number; she phoned someone else for it. Mike couldn't be reached on his mobile, so she left a message. In the evening, he rang back.

'Kate Griffiths? Hello, Kate. Haven't seen you for a while. What can I do for you?'

She was taken aback. It sounded like a response from the secretary of a film club she'd joined, long after her membership had lapsed.

'Well...'

'Don't tell me. Let me guess. Guy has asked you to ring me.'

'I... how...?'

'How do I know? Because you're the third person to phone from our lot. What's he playing at? I say "our lot", but we are a pathetic bunch these days, don't you think?'

'I'm sorry.'

'It's OK. I find it quite touching really. I don't even think it's nobody's business but mine. It's what friends are for, as they say. Are we friends – I mean our gang, the gang that used to be?'

'This is embarrassing, Mike. Honestly.'

He cleared his throat. 'Can I tell you something?' he asked.

'Of course.'

'In the old days, I spent most of my time summoning the courage to ask you out. I thought about you a lot. Wanted to be with you.'

'Then why...'

'Because I don't like uncertainty, the lack of immediate reciprocation.'

'What can a person do to make you certain, reciprocal?' She wondered if there were such a word.

'Be passionate, I suppose – about everything. I bet you never spent a minute summoning enough courage to ask me out.'

'You always intrigued me.'

'That's not the same thing. Anyway, enough of this. Look, I'm fine. Yes, I did throw a book at Lorna but I meant to miss. Yes, I did go AWOL for a few hours after she said she never wanted to see me again. Yes, I regret all that. Wait a minute – no, I don't regret it. Do you understand me?'

Kate looked around the flat. Night was falling. The street lights were stuttering on. Everything around her was dissolving in shadow. Only the mobile kept going, like some hospital monitoring apparatus registering her heartbeat, her helpless tremors, her racing blood.

'I don't know what to say.'

'Say you'd like to spend time with me.'

'I'd like to spend time with you.'

She wasn't sure where the words came from; it were as if he'd drawn them out of her. This was mad.

'OK. Look: it was good of you to ring. I appreciate it. Let's allow things to happen if they want to happen. By the way, you should tell Guy you rang.'

'I will. Are you serious, Mike?'

'Are you, Kate?'

She wanted to say, 'I think so'; but she said, 'Yes, I am.'

Once more, she didn't sleep well. She found that picture again, the one of a group of them. Mike, with just his head visible and wearing that serious, almost imploring, gaze, is in the background.

She could see now that in unposed shots of them all he was always the only one looking at the camera, looking at her, the one taking the picture.

Later, she couldn't remember whether she dreamt that she'd received a lovey-dovey bouquet of flowers or that she'd imagined it. She did recall an image from the dream: a toad, full of poison it was said, heaving itself dryly off the stage, into a pile of wet brown leaves.

Nor did she know if that crumpled ball of cellophane on the floor was part of the imagining or part of the dream. She did know that she faltered when reaching to pick it up, because it began to crackle open, like something exuding a life of its own, a small and slightly disconcerting upheaval that, once grasped, would have to be annihilated.

Lying on the bed, she loosened her jammies and lay provocatively into the night like someone ready to possess and be possessed in turn, someone waiting for completion and reciprocation.

At last, it felt right. She hoped it would feel right.

Outside there was a distant, short-lived clatter, followed ten seconds later by a shout: the fox dislodging something, she guessed, and being scared off by a neighbour. She stretched out at this external event, now rendered more vivid by some internal sense of wonder re-born and radiating through her body, leaving her shorn of sentiment.

# THREE MONTHS IN ANOTHER PLACE

Staring at the family burial plot of the Wordsworths at St. Oswald's in Grasmere, Cyrus Douglass hated even more the demon that had taken his hand, led him to the back of the chair on which Linda-Mo Reeves was sitting and placed it on her right breast. Linda-Mo hadn't complained or taken fright; in fact, her own hand hesitated on its way to holding or covering his in what he hoped might be an act of sanction. Nothing more had happened and nothing was said. It was three minutes to the end of the tutorial and it finished as it always had, with informal farewells and arrangements made for the next, though this time with no smiles.

After visiting St Oswald's, he thought he might have been, for want of a better term, the only black man in the Lake District that day. He'd stalled the changing nomenclatures of race; 'black' seemed as acceptable to him as 'white'. He knew there were others. When his fellow shufflers had got to the fence separating them from the Wordsworths and were debating which William was the famous poet, he was tempted to explain, but decided against. Except in a professional context, he was always nervous about disabusing whites of their mistaken notions, because his colour not so much neutralised his opinion as made their ignorance seem alien to natural feelings of superiority. It was well known back home in Kosciusco, Mississippi, for instance, that the most dangerous racists were whites who were no better off than their non-white neighbours. He sometimes felt sorry for them in a weird sort of way, since they'd mistaken the equality that might have revealed their error to them for their bad luck in having been socially downgraded. It was a subject, with reference to the literature of the Deep South, that he had been discussing with Linda-Mo Reeves before his lapse, if lapse it was.

He invoked the demon at that particular moment, there in the heart of Wordsworth country, because a paper he'd given to the University of Arkansas on the Lake poets had caught the attention of an authority at Harvard, who had subsequently urged the Arkansas authorities to send him on a three-month sabbatical to the Wordsworth Centre at Grasmere. He'd been in Britain for five weeks and had made contact several times with Julie Weaver, a local Wordsworth specialist based at Lancaster University. The reason he might not have made a good impression on her at their first meeting was the receipt of an e-mail message hours before from Maxwell de Ryan, his head of faculty and good friend back in the States. It was to do with Linda-Mo Reeves: she'd made a formal complaint about him.

Emboldened, the first thing he did was tell Julie Weaver. They were in a noisy Italian-style restaurant in Kirkby Lonsdale, a short drive from where he was renting a cottage above the town on the rise to Farleton Fell. (These names ever rang in his ears, echoing the multiple tinkle as Julie's loose silver bracelets tumbled down her arm each time she placed her elbows on the table. He loved the name of the place where he was staying – Hutton Roof.)

Their table was in a corner, away from the others. It was fairly busy in the dining area; but all the noise was coming from drinkers at the bar below. They could talk without being overheard.

'She's doing a Mamet,' he said.

'A what?'

He couldn't tell if she hadn't heard or were seeking explanation. She surely had heard of David Mamet. 'You know – the Mamet play about the sexual harassment of a university student by her tutor.'

At the word 'play', she'd begun to nod knowingly. Then she stared at him, her head cocked, her glass of wine suspended from a hand hanging pendulously. 'And?'

'Well, I've told you what happened,' he said. 'I don't deny it. All I can add is that, as you say so tortuously in your country, I had feelings towards her. Still have, I suppose, though if what Max says is true, perhaps any reciprocal interest, if it was ever present, has vanished. She's twenty, I'm thirty-two. Is that an unbridgeable gap?'

'Is she a bright student?'

'At this point in the conversation, I have to say that I think that's a woman's question. I don't mean that it's a woman asking it – it obviously is – but, with respect, that it's the sort of question only a woman would put at this juncture. I mean, the implication might be that first I find her attractive and then, maybe or maybe not, I discover she's bright, and if she isn't bright her grades will be elevated by her attractiveness and her response to my overtures, such as they are and if overtures they were. But yes – she's pretty bright; brighter than average.'

'It never happens with women,' she said, slightly diverting the exchange. 'One couldn't envisage a female teacher doing that to a male student.'

'That? What d'you mean, "that"?'

He felt he was already on the spot, or being encouraged to put himself on it. Despite the din, he could clearly overhear the conversations at tables close by if he concentrated, so he leant towards her; but as he did so she moved backwards, a like magnetic pole. He ignored the stares of bluff Yorkshire farmers' sons at his affront to normality.

'I think one could,' he said. 'But then we would have moved into different spheres, to do with active and passive motion. Do you know what researchers at the University of Wisconsin have discovered?'

She raised an eyebrow, smiled and leant towards him again, propping her chin on her left hand. Tinkle, tinkle, tinkle. He resisted any complementary movement backwards. 'No, I don't.'

'They found in a survey of divorcees aged between thirty-five and fifty that over seventy per cent of couples had experienced problems in their sex life based on confusion over who should initiate activity under the sheets, most of the men expressing regret at being expected to rouse the female and feeling injured at being thought of as unreasonable in their demands when arousal, hitherto unknown to them, happened to be off the agenda.'

His more chauvinistic colleagues, black and white, would call this 'congress talk' – a veiled overture to possible sex. He knew he wasn't free of chauvinism: it manifested itself when he least expected it, and his ever-ready resistance was no match.

She placed her hands together, as if in prayer: 'You – they – make it sound like a domestic chore.' And before he could jump in: 'Which, I suppose, for a lot of people is exactly what it is. Anyway, why did you do it?'

For a second or two at that moment, all the noise from downstairs coincidentally quietened, so that her query, expressed louder than in a normal speaking voice, rose above the immediate throng. Four tables away from them, heads turned, not in reaction to what had been said or that it had been said by a white woman dining with a black man but to the rise in decibels. 'It's not relevant or even a gripe,' he said, facing her as the hubbub and laughter resumed. 'But have you the remotest idea what it's like being the only black man in a white society? You must have heard that put another way. I mean, do you know how you'd feel being the only white woman in a community of blacks?'

'It would depend on what part of the world we were talking about. Lawless bloody Africa, for example. No go.'

'I don't really know why I did it,' he said, addressing her original question, head bowed. 'Today I blamed it on the devil, but that would be wishing my accomplice were my enemy. I wasn't trying to take unfair advantage. I just misjudged the situation, as men do. It's what we were just talking about – making the first move and all that stuff. If she'd clasped my roving hand and invited me to enter one of those other places with her, the problems would still be there but they'd be different.'

'Is there a racial element to it?'

'What do you mean?'

'Well, is it about a black man, or a man of colour, and a white woman as well about a man and a woman?'

'White woman?' He laughed out loud. 'Good grief, she's black! Linda-Mo Reeves is a woman of colour. And I, Dr Cyrus J. Douglass, am a married man. Dr Douglass and Dr Weaver – two doctors in the house and not the slightest fucking use to anyone.'

They both laughed at that. Diners around them laughed too, at other things.

'Oh, well,' she said, in a tone, he felt, that meant, 'Oh, well, that's different'.

She'd picked him up at the cottage and driven them both to town. The return journey in the dark on unlit serpentine roads seemed to take ages. The front of the cottage faced the hillside, not the town below and the distant fells. He made a point of not inviting her in, saying he was tired and had a few emails to send before going to bed. Although he explained how to reach the main road by driving straight on, she made a laborious five-point turn and re-traced her route. When she tooted the horn, it sounded like an affront in a place that had long surrendered to slumber. He went upstairs, got undressed and was soon asleep himself.

Next morning there was an email waiting for him from Max:

Hello Cy. Just a quick message to say that Reeves's complaint has gone upstairs but when they contacted her to make arrangements for a prelim she was evasive and said she'd be in touch later. I don't know what they meant by 'evasive'. By the bye, you're lucky – official contact with you will be through me. I've told the PTB (Powers That Be, you old framebreaker) that it's unreasonable to expect you to cut short your time in the UK and they agreed, though watch this space. I suspect you have L-MR's email address. I wouldn't contact her or her parents if I were you, unless she gets in touch herself. Actually, her parents have yet to make an appearance. She might try to reach you. Just be careful. STYS.

Scholars in England could handle critical theory from abroad as applied to the English literary canon; what they couldn't stand was biographical revelation and insight. It seemed to suggest an inability to discover what should be readily available on their own doorsteps. Perhaps few of them had been as geographically adventurous as William Wordsworth himself. In his preface to 'Annette Vallon: The Spirit of Memory', Douglass had told his Arkansas audience of the discoveries he'd made in France while investigating the story of Wordsworth's visit during the Revolution, his love for Vallon, the consequences of his having begat on her body a daughter, and his failure to bring mother and child back to England where he might have become a family man. And all this complicated by his love for his sister, Dorothy, and the probability that while on holiday in Goslar in the middle of Winter that love had become what English commentators still laughably described as 'absolute' (in short, they'd fucked).

But his time at the Grasmere centre spent in seeking more information about the Vallon relationship had been in vain. Countless others had presumably tried, though their lack of success in adding something to the voluminous literature was mirrored in his failure. There were other, more fruitful, gains. And he'd fulfilled a programme of talks, most of which had been delivered without notes. One was at a Penrith and North Lakes U3A meeting, another to A-level students at a Keswick comprehensive. Each all-white, though that more amused than angered him. He should be angry; he often felt angry. There was no antipathy as far as he could discern. But there never was from kids. He called it the 'Cassius factor' – after the way Muhammad Ali had made friends everywhere because of other, albeit manly, virtues. The context was wrong, his authority a deflecting characteristic.

The sabbatical had less than two months to run. He'd seen Julie several times since that first meeting in Kirkby, but always in a professional, if joshing, capacity. They'd had laughs, as the British said. She was a Lakes specialist, Southey mainly, a bit of Coleridge. She'd got the Lancaster authorities to pay for two lectures by him on Wordsworth, one of them titled 'The Waning Spirit; a Genius in Decline'.

He'd discovered correspondence between influential critics suggesting a conspiracy to bring the poet down. The gist of his talk was that what happened to Wordsworth happened to all zealots if they lived long enough. One or two brighter students disputed this, citing compelling examples of aged rabble-rousers. In reply, he said cryptically that the surroundings – he spread his arms to right and left – had a lot to do with it.

'Where this time?' she asked, he having phoned her for another dinner date.

'You could come here.'

Everything went dead. He thought about it. He thought about her thinking that he was thinking about it. They'd only ever eaten or had coffee in neutral places.

All the black person's fault lines had opened up to mantrap him: stares rapidly withdrawn, occasional muttered obscenities (but only from adults), and politeness severely conditional. He hated the term 'person of colour': it was again the white person's way of euphemising a separation from all non-white, and therefore inferior, cultures. He wasn't even sure about Julie Weaver. Their extra-curricular togetherness had doubtless been noted, commented on. Once, walking through her Lancaster department beside her, he'd had a sense of being flaunted (it happened sometimes with white women). Then there was her *faux pas* concerning Linda-Mo Reeves's skin colour. Somehow the moral ground had given her more secure purchase now that she could assign the problem to a region with its own rules – a lower, lesser region, perhaps.

She said yes; they agreed on a time; he offered to cook something Southern.

Just as he put the phone down, an incoming email pinged. He'd contacted his parents every week since his arrival. When the L-MJ business arose, he told them about it but had received no immediate reply. Three days later, as if they'd been working out what to say, their messages resumed. He'd tried to reassure them. His father emailed: 'Don't worry son; it'll be OK'. David Douglass Jr. only ever used 'son' when his attitude was ambivalent. He could see her from the kitchen. She'd 'made an effort' as the British also said. Her prematurely grey hair hung like a fell cataract about her shoulders. A petal-print sun dress was pulled up to reveal more of her shining bare legs than his Baptist parents would have thought decent. Make-up, hitherto eschewed in their dealings with each other, seemed to have transformed a latent, almost masculine sculptured beauty. She was helping herself to another glass of wine.

Before serving he tapped into the email. It was from Max:

Don't worry, my friend. It looks as though it's all over. She's met the PTB with her parents, at their behest apparently. Apologies all round, as they say. Will keep you in the loop. Love and friendship at all times. Xx

'Well,' she said, as they began to eat.

'Well what?'

He expected to have to tell more about the L-MR episode.

'Master Wordsworth and Mistress Vallon. Must they lie eternally secreted?'

He just raised his eyebrows.

L-MJ wasn't mentioned all evening. They talked of their academic specialties, laughing at the word 'specialism' and other American imports.

Despite having been out of place at St Oswald's that time, he'd found the locals friendly and welcoming if more curious than either. That was OK: it was curiosity that had led him there, defined one of his reasons for being. The Wordsworth Centre at Grasmere was a thirty-minute drive from Hutton Roof. He'd found the cottage in an accommodation list given him by the university and liked the name of the village; others too, such as Mardale, Kentrigg and Skybarrow Dodd, names sprung from the millennial earth and less obscure than Pascagoula, D'Iberville and Biloxi.

So he told her of an incidental find, concerning the name of the place where he was lodged.

'The local vicar here was the Rev Theodore Bayley Hardy,' he said. 'An army chaplain, a war hero.'

She pointed at something on his lip, placing the finger on her own to indicate the precise location. As he removed the blemish or whatever it was, her tongue slipped out to refresh her own lips, her mouth remaining open. There was a light lipstick stain on her teeth.

'Did he fight?'

That seemed to him like the wrong question, not a lecturer's clarification of terms.

'No, but he won the Victoria Cross; also the Military Cross. Your British medals.'

It was then that he knew she had postponed edification for something less certain, less capable of amounting to knowledge, more indisciplined and careless.

'He was also, goddamit, awarded the Distinguished Service Order.'

He spelled it out as a school-teacher would in the irritated expectation that it was filling a void, or revealing what a diminutive stood for. It was an age of abbreviation, that dignified label for a society that couldn't spell. It angered him. It was also a non-heroic age, with no foreign rumbling of the sort that Wordsworth could divine beneath his feet on Helvellyn. That irked him too, no less than the revolution that could go wrong, or lose its direction. He wasn't sure if Julie Weaver was friend or foe.

She downed her drink and re-filled their glasses, then took him by the hand and led him to the settee. They had never touched before, except to air-peck at each other's cheek. As she pulled up her dress to kneel on the cushions, he caught a stronger whiff of her apple-blossom fragrance, her pumiced freshness.

They had not talked about her staying but it was late when he tugged her towards the stairs. Inside, he was straining unseen towards some better judgement. But he joined her in her uncertainty and her carelessness and discovered what in the end amounted to solace and what could, given time, lead to something deeper.

'You see,' he almost whispered, as they lay crumpled in silence below the black oncoming fell, 'he was grieving for his dead wife and walked into the forbidden grounds time and again without a care for his own safety, while the bullets whizzed around him.'

'You mean the Reverend, in no-man's-land. So was he brave or reckless?'

It seemed to him, Dr Cyrus Douglass, like an academic distinction; and it seemed to her, Dr Julie Weaver, like an enquiry she would only make beyond a state of non-questioning, of mute communing and stilled speech. Both had the feeling of being in the presence of some more elevated state to which they might aspire if only it could be fixed and not remain eternally fugitive. It included Theodore Bayley Hardy and his far-distant and now soundless theatre of war, and Linda-Mo Reeves, who at that moment might have been wondering whether or not life's complications would ever go away.

*

Beside him, in bed, Julie Weaver snored. It was just a faint bubbling of breath, her mouth open, but now and then it would convulse, the shuddering almost waking her.

Who was she? Did she have someone, as the saying went, who also knew about the snoring, and was that person male, female, or of non-assigned gender (literary studies were for ever raking up new terms), and white or black?

Was she, in being with him, Cyrus Douglass – actually Cyrus Douglass III, but some detail was jettisoned without loss – cheating on the one she had or was it an 'open' relationship? Some terminologies seemed not old but outdated, the concepts they described having been found wanting or become enveloped in more accommodating, even warmer, words. Afro-American, people of colour. It didn't change attitudes.

Did Julie Weaver's life know tragedy and was it ongoing or had it been surmounted in exchange for the permanence of some wound kept hidden? (He remembered having struck 'ongoing' out of a Linda-Mo Reeves's essay on Faulkner, having described it, with thin conviction, as 'inelegant'.)

Did, she, Julie Weaver, would she, derive some hubris from her association with him, a man of colour, an Afro-American? Maybe in an office they'd passed on that saunter through her Lancaster department there'd been some good-natured but dowdy colleague in navy tights who would envy her, or imagine her to be a proxy in activities for which she was a non-starter.

He thought of Theodore Bayley Hardy, and what exactly he was doing out there high-stepping across barbed wire in that mudscape, a mad lone figure – there, then – pinioned by the sniper's crosshairs, the sniper's father a Württemberg Lutheran; so the sniper's trigger finger stayed for the English madman to continue his mud ministering; and the sniper smiling as he lowered his rifle and saw in the glass for a second an English clergyman rise heavenwards, an inside pocket full of Wordsworth's poems: *Er ist wieder da, Max!* Had he always worn his dog-collar out there? And poor Mrs Hardy. Had her husband done badly by her all their married life – the bed a place of anxiety, fear – and was all that business some crazy Flanders atonement?

Now he'd come to think about it, it was he who'd taken Julie Weaver by the hand and tugged her to the bedroom, each step without objection a token of her approval, like Linda-Mo Reeves's fluttering eyelids and silence as his hand had roved across her chest. He'd hated the encouraging fiend responsible only because the act had got him into trouble.

Long afterwards, he would recall it as 'the outpouring', those Cumbrian post-coital thoughts of a stretched but thin-populated sensorium aching for information.

Had it all been a misremembering? L-MR had apologised to him, so had her parents, they formally in a letter, and he was still teaching her. Questions, questions. The unassuageable desire for understanding people. They now smiled at each other a lot and shared coffee breaks. It was assumed that none of his other students knew about the Mamet moment that no longer was one. He'd noticed in her essays places where, a bit obviously, she'd used 'continuing' where she might have written 'ongoing'. He liked Linda-Mo. A lot.

While his university advertised that one of its staff had spent twelve weeks in Wordsworth country, it was awaiting the paper of which the fruits of the visit would be part. Not even Max knew about *O, how my ardour seeks the cooling covert stream.* Max de Ryan – grey-curled Uncle Remus descendant of an old plantation family from Heber Springs and true campus confidant. Nor did he know about his friend's line of research at the Wordsworth centre concerning a further cross-Channel visit by the poet, and the matter of Annette's sister, Françoise, who'd had an illegitimate child in 1798, acknowledged by her twenty years later.

Dr Cyrus Douglass had learned to keep things to himself. You simply couldn't trust anyone. In *académe*, as in the rest of a life wreathed by outrageous fortune, one was embattled, not knowing what anyone else thought. Were it not for access to a cooling covert stream, one might hit out and face a lynching of one sort or another. Not that his fellow gawkers in the graveyard at St Oswalds, Grasmere, that time would have given his explanation of which William Wordsworth was which anything more offensive than a distasteful shrug before moving on. Like finding more about William Wordsworth and his falls from grace, real and possible, one sought only progress, however slight.

# THE HILLSIDE DRIVE

Tonight there will probably be no reckoning.

I can see the old man sleeping in the corner bed as the five other patients on Bluebell Ward inspect their evening meals. What names! Bluebell – don't they know flowers wither? I suppose picking at food takes their minds off death and transience, except that here, just two storeys up, destinations represent little victories of a sort already lived through rather than portals to realms of abandon. These men have been recalled. When I'm not here, they shuffle along with tubes and bladder attachments outside their dressing-gowns in small acts of public bravery.

Harry Appleby – I've been calling him 'Harry' ever since I was twelve – has been talking fitfully during the previous two weeks, but tonight he is asleep, or feigning sleep. He has always feigned deafness, postponing for just a few minutes the obscurity of having to be a listener, gazing into the distance in the hope that his remoteness or indifference or suspension of good manners will return him to the centre of everyone's attention by default. He likes showing his best side. An amateur actor, he was once in *Dear Octopus*. I recall his spotlit monologue: 'We are an abstemious family.' Mum once said in rare tipsy company that she had married him because he looked like Ronald Coleman. To see him now, half outside the sheets with his knees drawn up and his Brilliantined hair falling about his head like shards of steel, requires me to wedge myself between the bed and the window, but there is barely room there for the slim charge nurse. I stay where I am, on the other side – the right side – of the bed and wonder whether this is how he looks as they approach him with the probe or whatever it is they examine him with so shamelessly. Foetal rather than contemptible. My contrast.

Where have we got to? Sitting up with his teeth in and hair combed, he has been filling some of the abysmal gaps in my memory; not his – that is all in place, ordered, supposedly there for the asking – but my own, full of splintered voices jostling in the ether. I am seeking belated epiphanies, Babel into message, and would always have called them that, in spite of my brother Ian's removal from such language. Yet so much has been shared.

In those days of fussy cotton dresses and snake-clip belts, I was aware of a jerking progress, a stuttering forward motion, as Harry Appleby, iron-founder, climbed out of the forge, put on a shirt and tie and a pressed suit and bought himself a book – an insurance man's ledger of premium-payers. (The 'Death Clubs' were still running then in the chapel schoolrooms. I remember the trestle-tables, the grim exchequer of trustees behind their columns of pennies – and my gran, each Saturday afternoon removing herself and her kind from the insult of a plain coffin and the pauper's send-off.) Then, after the 'book', the motor, some kind of bull-nosed matchbox with spoked wheels, the nose polished in proclamation of movement upwards, out of the ground, on to the flat. He loved cars; always called them 'she'. There was no flapping pennant but Harry's Woodbine had done duty for it as, sunlit, he stood with one foot on the running-board. We all moved in with my grandparents, from our thin, echoing council house. We inherited a drive.

Harry stirs, his free hand flailing backwards as if trying to locate something, someone, in a space that, unknown to him, no longer exists. Perhaps this often happens at home even now, ten years after mum's death. He lives alone in the same house, where inhibition and a certain looming futility clash in silence. It seems unfair that I should catch him like this, the unconscious embodiment of dependency, with its shocking loss of weight, of substance. He was once dashing in a cinematic, post-war kind of way. Then there was the relationship with my brother. 'Pity about Ian,' friends used to whisper, making their clumsy alliances with normality. Mum told of the aunt who had turned away from the pram (large and small wheels, like a locomotive) in revulsion at that huge, apparently pulsating, forehead. I have paid for being first-born and intact with the agony of self-reliance. 'Our June's A1 and can look after herself,' Harry used to say, pressing the back of Ian's head into the car's engine, where the workings of a distributor were being bonded in vain to a resistant memory.

I look around. Other visitors drift in. 'Why don't you get better?' the expressionless faces of some of them seem to be saying. 'As if we don't have problems of our own.' In the distance, I can hear the piping of the auxiliaries behind the food trolley. It is dark outside and trying to snow. At a high window beyond the ward a figure in a white coat stares down at us like a deity. Harry groans in his sleep. At least, I assume he is sleeping; perhaps it is another performance given to avoid the implacable scrutiny he would not have expected from mum. I can entertain all this. In the absence of his testimony or contempt, I can guess and form opinion. His meal, in its kiddies' plastic tray, lies half-eaten.

Loss of appetite, loss of faith. Whenever Harry scowls at the loose morals of the Sixties, I refer him to the Fifties and slashed cinema seats. It all began with Ian, snatched at every opportunity from mum's cradling to face the breezy emblems of what was new before he had been taught laboriously how the new worked, how it was powered. 'Fancy a run, Ian Appleby?' Harry would ask, burying a draught of cigarette smoke deep in his chest before expelling it, Coleman-like, through his nostrils. 'And you, our June – in the back.' The big ledger stayed at home like a bountiful queen bee and a smaller replica went with him on his rounds. It was a mystery to me then – all the entries against a list of names; the late night of accounting once a fortnight before a day spent at the office; the doorbell ringing at all hours; and his own house calls, often on a Sunday morning when mum was at chapel and Ian and I were running dizzy circles around grand-dad, the saturnine Grandpa Appleby. I often wonder how mum felt about exclusion. She was not part of the new, a forward-mover. Once a carnival beauty, she'd had her hour. Harry chose her and thereafter bathed in an equitable sea of tributes to his

75

good taste while she struggled weekly, on their one night out, to retrieve a vanishing sense of the world as oyster.

Stale sweat and hair oil – more memories. As Harry urged Bullnose along the twisting mountain road that Sunday morning, the double-edged scent trailed towards me and Ian on the back seat. We each occupied a corner, our legs stuck to the ribs of shiny green leather. When we took a corner, the indicator arm clicked up like an accusing finger. 'All right in the back, you two?' Harry asked, his eyes framed in the rear-view mirror, devoid of the expression required to make the question seem genuine. Neither of us answered, but looked up at the streaking world as if the car had left the ground. Now and then, Ian would climb into the space between the front seats and kneel awkwardly on the shaft housing while Harry held the crown of the boy's head in place without taking his eyes off the road, making it seem to me as if he were hoping against hope that the mountain air or the bumpy ride would work a miracle and the great skull would shrink to normal size. The final pull up to the row of wet-slate cottages was along a section of road pitted by oozing streams. Through the tilted windscreen came the whine of the engine and the squelch of tyres. Then the road merged into the vales and peaks of grassed tip-soil which crunched like ashes under baize when the car moved on to it. In each cottage garden a clothes-line strained with flags of white washing. The car stopped on a slope. Ian helped Harry ratchet the handbrake and then slid back into his corner. Through the windscreen we could see nothing between the bonnet and the garden gates. It was an effort to lean forwards, to ease ourselves upright. 'Stay there now,' Harry said. 'I won't be a jiffy.' His smoker's breath smelled of something bad that had taken hold in his mouth for ever.

He is coming around now, slowly aware of the state he is in and cursing himself, or me, for not clicking his teeth into place before the arrivals. He grasps his loose hair and sweeps it back, staring ahead like someone whose memory has momentarily failed him. I am still the stranger, still the one who weighs every thought before uttering it broadside. 'Is this what I made sacrifices for?' he's probably asking himself, assessing me unintentionally as something abstract or representative. (Everyone will have to take my word for all this: I'm in charge.) He is both proud and envious of me, and this duality is more agonising than the pity and loathing tossed together inside him by Ian's useless adulthood, by the boy in a grown-up's clothes. 'Does it hurt?' I ask. He frowns and nods. It is the manner of reply he reserved for Ian, who journeyed too far into his own province and lurked there stupidly, waiting for his otherwise healthy elders and betters to regress.

Perhaps this was where the gypsies lived. He had told mum about some hidden-away place where an old miner parted each month with a ten-shilling note to indemnify himself against damage to a frail Ford Popular. (I had pictured a row of squat dwellings with no back or front garden – a barge anchored in a slimy sea, its occupants sitting glumly below deck. 'I've told him,' he'd confided to mum. 'The diddicoys will have it jacked up if you're not careful.') I could see him heading into the wind with the red baby ledger under his arm. I pushed myself to the edge of the seat and watched him lift the latch of a wooden gate and pirouette onto a brick path. A woman with streaming honey-coloured hair stood in the doorway, her arms folded above a pinafore. I slid back and looked across at Ian. The wind was so strong, it was almost lifting the car. We could hear the hoarse bleating of sheep. Twenty minutes passed. It was too long, I realise now. Ian was sucking his thumb, and between his legs I spied the strange little tent rising and collapsing in the folds of his trousers. 'Where's dad?' he asked. Always questions, fearful questions. 'Sit still,' I told him. 'He said he wouldn't be long.' Ian inched forwards again, to get a better view. He began bouncing up and down with that brute impatience of his, but swung round and returned to his corner, knees first. I stared at the hurrying clouds. Then I saw a bead of light start to roll down the chrome bar above the bullnose, and the cottages beginning to sink slowly from view. Out of the side window, curious sheep glided past. Ian was already at the rear, watching the smooth rim of the crater juddering towards us. I wanted to scream but couldn't. As we rumbled to the edge and just before we tipped up, I turned and saw the tremor of my father and the blonde woman racing down the slope. He blamed me, of course. For not restraining my daft brother. We crawled out. Ian the survivor, soon to be dead, but not because of a car accident.

I have words for things now. It was what he wanted for me, Ian having been consigned early to shuffling through tar for the rest of his days. They are an irritable lot on Bluebell Ward, Harry included. They look abandoned. One or two of the chattier ones might build a fraternity, given time, but there is too much coming and going and too vain an atmosphere for sympathy to flourish. I ask myself how I can be so harsh. Like me, the other women visitors do their duty, barely disguising an instinct that to be confined is to be considered unmanly by those whose distress they come nightly to alleviate. Most of the men put on a show: Harry Appleby is not the only actor. But soon, hitched up to conduits and reservoirs, they will begin roaming abroad with their secrets under the dim lights. I turned up early and unexpectedly one afternoon, before anyone else, and saw him on the move at the end of the corridor, walking away from me in a sad enactment of a whispered prognosis. If he were here, Ian would know none of this; instead, he would screw up his face with the effort of trying to accumulate his father's pain. It is only now, when Harry Appleby can adduce burgeoning mortality as a further reason for keeping things to himself, that I wait for the moments of confession, for the splutterings of truth. It is I who have learned to construct, after all. Con rod, big end, piston, side-valve. So that I do not have to tramp the streets seeking the sundry payments of debtors, he has insisted that I learn a subtler naming of parts. Suddenly, as though I am not there, he cries out for the nurse.

The swish of the curtain excludes me. It is an end to putting things together. For another day. But we could have died. Christ, he could have killed us.

# THE VILLAMOURA LONG-DISTANCE SEA-SWIMMING CLUB

She once stood for thirty minutes in the rain outside Cineworld, just to see him.

Well, she was sheltering where he couldn't see her, but it was cold, with the downpour dampness trying to get at her skin like the palm of his hand, she imagined, as it breached her cardy and arrived at cotton and elastic, the last flimsy redoubt on its journey south.

One Saturday afternoon, when she knew he was going in to town with his pals, she stalked him, stopping to look into a shop window of disability aids when, up ahead, they bumped into someone she didn't recognise and stopped to banter. The woman inside the shop stared at her, then cocked her head to one side and smiled a sickly smile, as if she thought the sixteen-year-old girl looking in had a disease that would see her in a wheelchair before she was twenty. Her Aunty Joyce was sixty-three at the time and had MS but she'd been fighting it, as if it were a violent lodger she couldn't get rid of who mostly played loud music but who sometimes came in drunk and bounced off the walls like a pinball.

Then she trapped him.

It was at the Bethesda schoolroom one Friday night when her friend Lorna from just down the road was ill and couldn't go. Only a couple of them went to chapel. The woman minister opened the youth club to anybody in the hope they might attend Sunday service. It never happened. They all played table-tennis and pool and milled around. Rob called it 'the last youth club in Christendom'. Music played, 'heathen music', he called it. When she grinned at that he saw her, and his gaze lingered longer than her recognition warranted. It wasn't recognition, he would tell her later, it was complicity. Most of them were heading for exams and loved their subjects. They didn't 'do' drugs and despised those who did and those who didn't want to understand Shakespeare and get on. Rob was good for four A stars. He didn't live near her, it was the opposite direction, so when they all left that evening to walk home, she sidled up to him and played her Lorna card.

It was getting dark.

Lorna always walked home with her, she said.

'I know. I'll go with you.'

He couldn't have known because it wasn't exactly true. That was Rob.

He needed no excuse save that written on their still-alive feeling of collusion. That word 'heathen' uttered with a knowing smile had suggested knowledge of a province to which they were both strangers, but a province of rebellious familiars in retreat from stupidity and stuffiness.

She liked his company. Walking side by side that evening, they now and then bumped against each other.

She told him the contact sparked access to his four-stardom. They laughed. She might get one star, Miss Harrison had told her, if she worked hard; she might even get an additional A for English. French was, well, *une ligne de démarcation* as to whether she'd get any grade at all.

They messaged each other a lot after that, after school was over, in the evening. Her long emojis and stickers trailed from the high billowing kites of her endearments. He usually managed one upper case X before dropping to a couple of lower case kisses.

He sent her a poem by Donne:

*If they be two, they are two so*
*As stiff twin compasses are two,*
*Thy soul, the fix'd foot, makes no show*
*To move, but doth, if th' other do.*

He wasn't a keen texter, preferring to send her links to subjects he thought might interest her. For long periods – well, days – she'd hear nothing from him. 'I've been maintaining radio silence,' he said, the first time it happened, but didn't say why or explain to her what it meant. The links didn't usually interest her much, but she accessed them anyway and in reply offered what her grandparents would have called 'her fourpen'orth'. She never knew if he thought her comments interesting or original; at least, he never said, just nodded. Nodding could mean anything.

One day he sent an attachment with the message: 'Hi Millie. Do you like this guy?'

It was a drawing of Herodias, by Aubrey Beardsley; an illustration to *Salome*, the play by Oscar Wilde. Miss Harrison had given them a talk about Symbolism, mentioned Beardsley as a representative Brit, and then passed swiftly on – as she always did whenever a 'cock & balls' illustration might be on the way, which is how one of her A-level art class described it. She'd told Rob about the talk but he'd evidently forgotten. That was Rob, too. It was the picture in which a tits-out Herodias is attended by an homunculus on her right and an androgyne on her left, the latter with a comical stubble of pubes and wearing a wig. Rob had drawn a cartoon bubble arising from the mouth of the downstage character sort of leaning out of the picture frame, wearing a mask, looking at the viewer and introducing with an outstretched hand the weird goings-on behind him – it. Rob had typed: If you think this lot are odd, you should meet my family.

She didn't think it was particularly funny. Nor could she work out if it were an invitation or a deterrent. But she did meet his mother and father – eventually. Also some eccentric aunts and uncles. And even when she did, their opinion of her was impossible to work out. The mother was thin, nervous, and fussed over her as if for the sake of it, talking thirteen to the dozen; the father was mostly silent, as though the pipe he smoked demanded all his concentration. The mother used to be a teacher (she never found out about the 'used to'), and the father designed kids' toys – Rob, smirking, showed her a catalogue of them, big bulky plastic things. The two looked old enough to be Rob's grandparents. They'd had him late. Like the toys, they both seemed to have been left behind in a previous generation.

Millie got an A in her main subject and scraped a pass in the other two. It was enough for Falmouth College of Art. Stellar Rob sailed into Balliol on first interview to do English.

Thereafter, as one of her friends was to put it, she gave chase while he played the vanishing quarry. She knew he was losing interest when in his messages he began calling her 'Mill'.

'WTF is Mill' she replied the first time it happened, dropping the interrogative, as Rob called it.

He didn't answer. Not answering made him appear doubly superior: he wasn't going to apologise and he wasn't ready to explain.

Millie was undeterred; but the next three years leavened whatever was growing between them to just friendship, punctuated by weekends among dreaming spires or Cornish sand-dunes.

Once, in an Oxford pub in their second year, she asked him where he thought they were going. He could have made a joke but didn't.

'I know where I'm going,' he replied. 'Where are you going?'

She stared at him, suppressing anger.

'Do you know what that sounds like?'

With his finger he twirled the top of his glass: 'No. What does it sound like?'

'It's as if you think I don't know what I want for myself.'

'Does it? Do you?'

She should have said she didn't. It would have been the truth. But it was also true that she wanted him to understand the meaning of 'we': both of them as a pair, not as individuals following their own paths away from each other.

A second time, closer to finals, they were in a café at Mousehole. She stared through the window at the grubby harbour – it 'smelled' of rotting shellfish – and the mist lurking on the horizon, and the caked sauce bottle on the table, the stained and dog-eared menu.

'Tell you what,' he said, leaning across and taking her hands in his. 'We should make a vow after all this is finished that we go away together.'

'You mean a holiday?'

'Kind of. But permanent. With a view to permanence.'

'What – settle down?'

'In a manner of speaking.'

He sounded mysterious, unconvincing. Word was that he would get a 'first'. The paintings and supporting stuff she was preparing for her degree show weren't bad, but they weren't brilliant either.

The word proved to be correct; and she emerged with her BA, 'like all the others', as she's fond of describing it.

They did go away: on a rail tour of European capitals, paid for by his parents and her savings from weekend stints in a Falmouth restaurant. All the time she made plans for them in silence, so as not to pressure him – what job she might go for (teaching, possibly), what kind of accommodation they could afford, where they might settle. 'I suppose I was trying to anticipate him,' she confided to a college friend, 'thinking I knew what he wanted for us; if it was for us that he wanted it, if you see what I mean. It was the last stage, you understand, of my pursuit.'

At which point she laughed.

It wasn't the last stage, but it was in Paris, towards the end of the trip, that she saw the light. (That's been a frequent joke, too.) She knew, before he could admit it, how any liking he had for the conventional was already being subverted, giving his need for the ordinary its desperation as well as its ambivalence. She'd never seen two men kissing before. She put it like that rather than say that one of them was Rob. It must have resulted from some lightning connection he'd made when he was out alone. Rough trade, she supposed, a description she'd only read about. The details didn't concern, nor did the idea that not everyone was open about everything, even then, and least of all those matters that were unresolved. She didn't mention it to him, and she knew that if they split up his reason for doing so might be unconnected with the scene she'd witnessed. Or it might be a bit of both. There'd be bravery in it, and the dubious pleasure of knowing the truth behind what was yet to be divulged.

He found work with a government department in London, and they saw less and less of each other. She'd begun trying to make a living as an artist. It was tough, impossible really. In the December after they left college, she phoned him.

'Remember the time you asked me where we were going?'

'I think so.'

'I have an answer.'

'And it is?'

'Our separate ways.'

He didn't respond.

'But we should get together for Christmas,' she said.

'Of course. We should.'

And they did. Not significantly with her family or his but with their school gang. It was like a return to the old jostling, to the beginning. She felt a renewed prompting of pursuit, especially as the women, the ones who didn't go away for three years and were now settled in jobs and smoking cigarettes, seemed to be enticing him with new-found allure.

Then, in the New Year, he vanished. Almost literally. He sent her a text saying that he would explain later. His family told her he'd left his job and decided to go 'walkabout', whatever that meant. It was a dismissive term. They seemed to feel cheated of respect. He'd promised to contact them but a month passed and they'd heard nothing; nor had she. He then sent two postcards, one from France, one from Portugal. His father showed them to her, his pipe smoke billowing in his anxiety while his wife fretted in another room. The messages on the back didn't reveal much, expect to say that he was fine.

'Has he not texted?' she asked him.

He looked puzzled, as though not knowing what texting was, or believing it to be an inappropriate method of communicating things of importance. Had his son confessed, she wondered.

She received another message: 'I'm in Olos d'Agua. Come on out. You could get a plane to Faro.'

After looking it up, she scraped the money to fly economy and he promised to meet her. But he wasn't there. When she phoned him he said something had cropped up and asked her if she could get to Olos, where he'd meet her on the sea front. She did – but he wasn't there either. She realised it was the first time she'd heard him speak for months. The 'sea front' at Olos was a mere cove, overlooked and almost threatened by a cascading tourist metropolis.

In despair she climbed a path through the fire-red cliffs that gave sight, in the distance, of some kind of resort with a marina. A passing Brit said he thought it was Villamoura. She repeated the name, 'Villamoura', like an explorer within striking distance of a long-cherished destination, some Eldorado. Villamoura's inviting whiteness shivered in the haze.

She sat down on her rucksack, wondering if the fact that she'd got this far meant she'd passed some test of independence and, having passed, was now entitled to regret that she'd ever agreed to be examined. She'd never asked, 'WTF is happening to me?' She didn't use 'WTF' very often.

Out at sea and moving in her direction from left to right was some sort of commotion: or rather a dozen pools of commotion moving slowly as one, a pattern, almost floral, about half a mile out. She looked for the informative Brit, but he'd gone and was now a white blob down below, negotiating some steps and clinging to a shaky wooden rail. Shielding her eyes, she could see that the little areas of tumult were swimmers, each wearing a black bathing cap, and for all the world giving a synchronised performance. It didn't look like a race; at least, not until the lead swimmer appeared to be edging away, turning towards even deeper water. Then the lead completed 180 degrees and began heading back for El Dorado, the others following in due course and keeping their distance, moving at an easy pace. They appeared to be at home in their dangerous element, and she watched them until they were out of sight.

Before they turned, she saw something appear on the horizon out of the mist, like some blue Atlantis. For just a few seconds the swimmers seemed to be heading in its direction. But it disappeared again when they began making for home. She re-saddled her rucksack and returned to the cove. Later, she took out her mobile and let Rob's number ring unanswered before leaving a half-petulant message, wondering if she would ever call a halt to the chase or whether her quarry would grow tired of being pursued.

She remembered to watch out for the wallet-thieves, who, it was said, came from Faro to Albufeira and Olos to perform their slippery acts of dispossession.

A few months on, she would smile at what she'd seen and what she'd done. Perhaps she'd imagined it all: image and thought were far enough gone to have been wishful.

And she wondered if she might send him a Donne poem, too: a more relevant one, more easily understood; A GCSE one, not an A-level star one, like his:

*No man is an island*
*Entire of itself,*
*Every man is a piece of the continent,*
*A part of the main.*

If only she knew where he was, what had become of him. And, like the fabled city exploding out of the waves, would he stay around long enough for her to beach herself on his shores?

# TRAVELS IN LAKELAND

It was an aimless sort of drive to Cartmel. There was nothing to do any more. No future beckoned. As a prelude to a sort of oblivion, it couldn't have been bettered.

I glanced across at Bill in the passenger seat. He was, as they say, in a world of his own. Not mine, anyway. Although, in a sense, ours was one world; we'd just begun placing markers in different regions of it; that was all. We'd exchanged few words since leaving. The silences of compatibility had become the lacunae of estrangement and bitterness. We were both academics; we had the words.

But it was the children, you understand. Not ours, who didn't exist, but ones who might exist and be ours if only we could agree: children we could bring into the world, as they also say. Our world. I still use the present to discuss things that I once thought would probably never be.

The sun streaming through Bill's open window revealed the fine honey-down on his arm. I'd noticed it before, of course; it would catch the breeze and shiver like an ecstatic spasm or a field of wheat. But, in short, we'd had a row, perhaps the final one, or so it seemed at the time. He won't have his say in this, of course – I won't let him – and no doubt he had a lot to unburden. But perhaps not.

The land gradually flattened out from the tail of its legendary attractiveness, as though leaving the sound and bustle of lakeside devotees behind, like folk abandoned to their unsuspected fates.

Now and then, the great bay could be seen steelily glinting, the one that had claimed the lives of those exploited Chinese fishermen trapped by the tide. Immigrants – the word had picked up such detritus of late.

But local Cantonese restaurants weren't viewed in the same way after that, nor indeed were the incongruous Chinese themselves in their breaks from nightly flash-frying. In an odd way, the drownings did the survivors a favour by raising and disseminating an uncharacteristic desire to take pity and understand. The Poles, their newspaper signalling to them among the home-grown 'blats' and their one shop looked after by a girl with big triangular earrings made from ersatz stained glass, were hopefully included too, but good will is always limited and short-lived.

Cartmel. The name always seemed to appear for no reason, just a place at the end of nowhere. Wasn't there a Priory? A racecourse was recalled, an unlikely venue that never appeared in the runners-and-riders lists, unless you were a local. Then there was a posh restaurant with a Michelin star or two and a reputation for being an establishment that served food you wouldn't much like and couldn't afford in a Brigadoon village you might not be able to find.

I let the car roll into the centre and parked next to the racecourse. The place seemed populated by old couples; older than us anyway, their children grown up and with children of their own: the ever-flowing stream of lineage and descent. Yet out of nothing can come nothing.

The bookshop built into the medieval arch was closed for no offered reason, though the spines of its wares spoke mutely to the frustrated browser through small windows to which they crowded like Derek Mahon's mushrooms in that disused Co. Wexford shed ('So many days beyond the rhododendrons/With the world waltzing in its bowl of cloud') – *A Lune Valley History*, *Southey's Table Talk*, *Fishing For Sea Trout In The Hodder*, *The Cavendishes Of Holker Hall*. The more we read, it seems sometimes, the less we learn. The pub, all exits open, was evacuating night's reluctant miasma; the swish restaurant, serving no lunches, was exclusivity behind glass, a place for peering into, eyes shielded.

We still said nothing.

But there was a beckoning, some Nemesis, some reminder. So we walked to meet it as though guided by an unseen hand.

In this way we came to the Priory, really a church masquerading, and at its stern we saw a walked-over flagstone, some inscribed grey slate of bulk, telling of the Son who drowned, like those latter-day hired Orientals, on June 13, 1782, at Lancaster Sands, and his Mother, who drowned at the same place a year later to the day.

O Grief, where was thy swift effacement? You take us up and urge us to the shore, where we approach the coming bar, its vast out-riding swathe already filling our footprints from below.

'Isn't that extraordinary?' Bill said at last, staring transfixed at the uneven floor and its proclamations risen from the depths. *De profundis.*

I nodded, and he saw me nod. And I saw him watching me nod. At what?

Not long after, we left. The plight of others had moved us. We would never forget it. Not that coming night, nor any other night in the never-ending ebb and flow of our blood.

perrer, peara, appel, aple pearer, apple, apple, apple, parerer, parer, apple parer, apple parer. Paring an aple, paring an apple, paring an aple, paring an apple.

Mr Gant come to day an Her Majusty tikt me off for gone to see im an me only takin the time I was entitld too. I was standed by the stabell door becuase I could'nt see Mr Gant from the kitchin window and he was hear to currycome Major as he explined it to me for I had nevver see any persn currycoming a horse as big as Major before and as I'am standing there by the stabell door and pearin in he is puffn and gruntn an tellin me as what currycoming does and it's like this you take a currycome and curry him all over his body, an that is too raise the dust, beginnin first at the neck, holding the left cheek, of the headstall in the left hand an curry him from the setting-on of his head all over the body to the buttuks down to the point of the hock, an then change your hands, and currycome him before, on his breast, and, laying you're right arm over his back, join you're right side to his left, an curry him all under the belly near the fourbowls, an so all over from the knees and back upwards after that, go to the far side and do that agin likwise. If he did bless me Majors thing began to grow down longer and it was pink like a pigskin but smooth as a shammy lether and with brown spots like the livver ones on the back of olde ladys hands Mr Gant saw me as I was listenin and he took old of Majors thing in his tow hands and wiggle it about smilin as he did so and I turned an ran strayt into the arms of Mr Robert the Footman. Her majusty saw us and called me back to the kitchin didnt I have anythink bettr to do she said an I lookt back and see Major hopping like he was mad and steam was comin outoff his nostrils it was so cold that mornin as I was startin early but Majors thing had gone back a littl bit into it's lethern pocket. Her majusty askt if I had got use to the new apple parer I said yes and I thohgt it was bettr than standin their watchin the peel grow down form yer hands like Majors thing groin longer which made me smile.

Mr Robert he is teaching me to read an write and spell so here is the copied down list of all here at Coleford Lacey, —

The Master, The Mistress, Miss Catherine.

Margaret E. Britton Lady's maid

Emma Collite Housemaid

Charles Cooling Groom who is ill and Mr Gant who is coming from Leddington Hall to do his work

M. Robert Davis Footman he whose teeching me

Elizabeth Davy Laundry Maid,

Maria Ellison, Housekeeper who is Her Majusty an is nowne has Mrs tho she is spinnister

Amelia Jane Fry Parlour Maid

Emily Harris Kitchen Maid for she is me

Matilda Koch a Gest who is from Germeny

Elizabeth Roberts Head Cook
Margaret Smethwick, Cook
Walter Jenkinson Head Butler
William Thompson Butler
Elizabeth Watkin, Laundry Maid
Lucy Young Housemaid

Mr Robert has teached me to write apple parer. Apple parer. Its new an a beuatifull object and so is the new egg wisk from Amirica so beuatifull that I do keep starin at them much to Her Majusty's annoyince saying theirs laudrin needed to be soaked an blued an washed and rinst, rinst agin, rung out, an hunged to dry and then ironded as if I did'not know. Mr Robert he says Emily Harris you noticed to much fer you're own good. Mr Robert says Mr Gant laernt evry thing from Mr Charles Cooling Groom and Mr Cooling isn'ot long fer this worrld but not to hold a horses thing in the present of a woeman – an Mr Gant dont wash hands in fair water an rub him all over while they'are wet, as well over the head as the body an last, take a clean clothe an rub him all over again till he be dry then take another hairclothe, an rub all his legs exceeding well from the kneese and hoks downwards to his hoofs, pickin an dressin them very carefly about the fetloks, so as to re-move all gravl an dust which will lie in the bendin of the joints and so as to make Major all over shinin like a chesnut conker.

Today I see Miss Catherine on the back lawn an her dress blow in the wind witch shews her babby soon to be born and her with no husband oh the sadnes when all should be joyfull Mr Robert sais the Mistrees is be side her self and her husban the Master he speeks to us no more but I hered him shoutin after mid nite an it was far away in this big house and waked me up and frighten me.

The harvist is got in.

Culander, collander, colander, colander colander. Stair case, candlstick, candlestick.

My name is Emily Harris, I am twenty-five years of age and I am from Worcestershire, is what Mr Robert writ down fer me to copy it. To day Miss Koch she is walkin upandown the terris agin reading her reglar letter from home with meny pagess an her face all creesd like the plowed field at Pendlborough.

Mr Robert took me an Miss Watkin, Laundry Maid an Miss Young Housemaid to Mr Coolings room were he is lyin loking up with is arms foldin like the knites in side St Cutheberts where they're of stone an as still believe me as Mr Cooling is still unner his clean sheet an waitin too goe too St Cutheberts hinsef. Miss Watkin is sobbin but try and not too make us here but I looks and she as a hankecheif unner her noise an her hand is so rore from laundrin that is crackt becuas her hankecheif is red with blod as like her noise is bleedin Mr Cooing he is yeller has tallo an he sais no thing. Mr Robert tuches is sholder. There their in that room be no other culours cept red and whit an yeller as fer as my eye's tells me. I was they're when the Nurse that comes in afrom Daglingnorth to give Mr Cooling a bedwash gave him a bedwash and I coodnt help but look up from my duty and see him all rubed down as if he were his own Major in the stabel and, so, I did smile at that an the Nurse caugt me smileing and frowned at I like Miss Koch reading on of her long leters from home.

Winter is a'comin an now wea're litenin all the fires at Coleford Lacey wich is extrer an we are risin erlier in the morn now at five an thirty an as wellas makin fer Mrs Britton Ladys Maid her tea at six of the morning promt, the lamps too clean and full on each an everyday and carryin more water up three stayers to the third were the famlys bed roms are and they all want fires now specally Miss Catherine. As fer the fires they have to bee kept alit an as wellas the water there is now the coal Tonihgt I was all most to tirde to undress but I look out off the window and see the stars and everything roun Coleford Lacey coverd by frost sprinkld over everything and its all is baeutfull has anything Ive ever seen.

Mr Robert as got me to prectice these an hear I write them down not lookin

My mother was named Bessie and she is dead.

My father is named Thomas and he is in the Workhouse at Droitwich.

It is my birthday on November the 23 rd and I shall be twenty-six years of age. I think my father is fifty-eight years of age. His left arm was crushed in a thresher and he cannot work – I have no brothers or sisters –

apple parer, colander, whisk,

thresher, candlestick, tureen

staircase, bellows, gin trap, copper bedwarmer

Brougham, vixen, cock pheasant. hen pheasant

Minié rifle – the Master's favourite and folk come round specal to see it

Mr Gant he as not com an Miss Eizabeth Roberts Head Cook sais he must have bin out to late at the Kings Head prevous nihgt Miss Roberts as I tolde you so look on her face fore she was agin Mr Gant comein to standen for Mr Cooling.

Consommé whitch is Frensh Mr Robert says an shews me how too writ it, though I have sen it made no endof times but did not now how to spell it. Consommé, consommé, consomeé. Mr Robert he stays to talk to me some, about my father who gets my wages.

Miss Koch as came over from Germeny to keep Mis Catherine compny is now to go back there and we knows not why but must be the letter's she reads as make her look so sad and deed all is of a turvy because the Honrable Mr Charles Poulton from Colesbourne who was Miss Catherines reglar genleman visiter is not come now since Miss Catherine is off childe as they says and her babby can be seen growing under her dresses, a little bump it is. Mr Robert says he onse saw Miss Catherin and the honrable Mr Poulton on the south lawn and Mr Poulton he did take Miss Catherins hand and did kiss it so daintly but Mr Robert says thatbe histry and now Miss Cathrine will have no husband as she would have ben happy with and the Master would stop his shouting at night. It do all remind me of what evryone is saying cept Wm. Thompson Butler, who wouldnt say it because he is the one it's said about, that as he Wm. Thompson Butler is the father of Miss Catherins baby and I can say something but am afeared as I saw Mr Wm. Thomspon come out of the nursery on the third floor all of an agitasion where Miss Cathrine had gonein and did not come out til I saw her when I was out of sihgt and her hair had come undone and she was a'patting it back and walking away from me and smothing down her dress, this was when the Master and Mistress was away at Coln St Aldwyns and I was upstair cleaning out the Mistresss' sewingroom where I don't go much, O this World.

I am all confusd as Wm. Thompson Butler was with the Master in the war and would be shorely smited by the Master if he dicovrd his secret if, it realy does be a secret but why Mr Thompson and Miss Catherin could not be happy together I dont know Today we are all eating and lisning to Mr Jenkinson Head Butler tell funny tales from the market at Cirencester but poor Mr Wm. Thompson is staring at his plat of vittels and pushin his green's round like a hand out in the field a'turnin the newmoan grass. An then Her Majesty she says as Mr Gant he's not coming aftr all to took over from poor Mr Cooling god pertect his soul an I wonders if it's to do with Mr Gant holdin Majors thingumy like he did afore me and me red in the face and all. Mr Robert tells me agin Mr Cooling is not longfor this worrld.

Mr Robert knocked at my door late so gentle this evenin, if Her Majesty knew thered be ruckshns but he comes to give me lesons and spelling and this is what he tells me to copyout,—

101

Is not Miss Emily Harris the most perfect of God's lovely creations?

He says it is a rhetorical queston and he write out rhetorical for me and explaining how it is a queston that do not have an anwser and while I frowns, as not understanding like Miss Matilda Koch when shes a'reading her long letters from home in Germeny Mr Robert he kneals afore me and touch my cheek so gentle like and I took his hand and put it on my breast, and I felt it was just the start but there was a noise below we could both here it and we went out Mr Robert first and then, Her Majesty tells us all that poor Mr Cooling has past on and then the Master and Mistress and Miss Cathrine come down in their silk gownes to tell us what Her Majesty has just told us, and the Master he makes a long speech, but all I could see was Miss Cathrines little bump which she was holding tender just like Mr Robert had touchd my cheek and my breast with it's neb allmost hurtin me with it's hardnss.

Each night afore I put this book away for I cannot speke to my father I think of him settlin down in the werkhouse and all of them under their blanketts and there breathe like smoke all a puffin into the night, and I pray for all the misfourtn in the worrld to sleep as a babby and wake in the morn happy and waitin for the currycome like Major, combin all the bad out and the currycoming bein done properlike and, not as Mr Gant of Leddington Hall does it makin lihgtof the worrld that has so much sadness init.

# THE RETREAT TO LE CATEAU

*What though the field be lost?*
*All is not lost; the unconquerable Will,*
*And study of revenge, immortal hate,*
*And courage never to submit or yield:*
*And what is else not to be overcome*
Milton, *Paradise Lost*

Some things are remembered because long afterwards they make you shiver. That Saturday afternoon phone call from the funeral director, for example, after my grandfather had died. 'I'm with him now,' he told my father, sounding like someone who'd come across my grandfather after he'd wandered off, his mind a mess. He'd already taken the body to the Chapel of Rest. Of course he was 'with him'.

There was nothing wrong with my grandfather's mind in that sense; or my father's, come to that – or anything else about my father's that years of prodding the language as a university lecturer couldn't have corrected, despite an addiction to home-brewed ale.

'Funeral director be buggered,' he muttered to some invisible accomplice after replacing the receiver. 'He's a mortician. A bloody mortician. What does he want now?' My father believed that one Americanism was worth a dozen British euphemisms. 'I should bloody well hope he is with him. He was three hours ago.'

What this undertaker told my father had everything to do with the Great War. My grandfather was then Captain Horace Lennox, who won the Military Cross for gallantry during the battle of Mons. I'd heard my grandfather described as 'a wild one', a 'jack-the-lad'. I could have worked it out myself, but I was in my twenties before I discovered that he had married my grandmother because she was pregnant. I knew that even my older sister's legitimacy was only guaranteed by the decision of my mother and father to marry after the event. It's a common enough situation now, marriage often not considered at all, but whereas my parents decided on a quiet Register Office ceremony, my grandfather had mocked the prudes by insisting on a full and formal white wedding, its guest list stuffed with sundry mistresses (we now know), and boozy relatives and companions, while my grandmother's family dis-burdened him of any shame, such as it was. You can tell from some of the photographs, in which her side wears almost mournful looks.

As to the war, my grandfather was as proud of his namesake and commanding officer, General Horace Smith-Dorrien, as he was of his medal.

Following defeat at Mons, the British Expeditionary Force and the allied French army were harried south towards Paris by the triumphant Germans. Smith-Dorrien, a career soldier and veteran of the Boer War, ordered his two corps companies to stand and fight. My grandfather, who once told me that Smith-Dorrien had winked at him during a brief visit to the Front, was with the second corps. Through the villages of Montroeul, Boussu, Paturages, and Frameries, the second managed to stall the German advance, despite being outflanked on one side. Unlike those First World War survivors who were reluctant to talk about their time in the trenches, my grandfather was full of it. At one stage, I'd learned more from him than I had from books and TV documentaries, but not of the action that had earned him the MC.

'Your father will tell you about that,' he said. 'And ask him, too, about that daft angel.'

He gave the impression of revelling in some aspect of armed struggle that was beyond patriotism; but it was not as shallow as mercenary. If I call his attitude mischievous, it's only because no other description fits. There were further instances.

When I was twelve, my grandfather took me to our docklands area where there was a famous transporter bridge spanning the river; it was a monumental structure of iron and steel with a suspended gondola travelling between the two banks. A gondola ride was tame and short-lived. But it was possible to climb one stanchion of the bridge, walk across the top, and descend the other side. The bridge's appearance was skeletal, resembling something fixed but unfinished. It took us almost forty minutes to cross. His age – sixty – and mine meant that we had to stop every few minutes to catch our breath, though I believe now that, having discovered his element in some strange way, he'd been stopping just for me. At the very top we must have appeared dwarfish from below. The higher we climbed, the stronger and more noisily the wind blew, and when we were half way across he placed his hands on my shoulders and pointed me downriver from where the wind was rushing at us. Its force made a permanent 'O' of my mouth. What scared me was not so much the height or the blast but the impression I had that he'd taken two or three steps back to leave me exposed. The memory is still vivid, something I sensed at the time but did not witness, until of course I turned to see him back there, grinning in an odd manner and with his coat collar turned up. My mother and father were furious, which is what he wanted: having lost his parental authority, he aimed to subvert his son's and daughter-in-law's. I can still hear our steps on the metal, his presence high up on that day no consolation for the fear and loneliness I felt.

My mother was angrier about the bridge episode than my father, who by that time had already begun drinking heavily and would absent himself from awkward family scenes. I marvel at how my father kept his job until normal retirement age. One of his ways of atonement was to sit with me and read me stories, or tell me of the incident outside Frameries, as my grandfather had predicted, or maybe suggested.

'What's the daft angel?' I remember asking.

I told him this is how my grandfather had referred to it.

'That was the Angel of Mons,' he said. 'A book author called Arthur Machen made up a story about an angel appearing in the sky when your grandfather and his soldier friends were being chased by the Germans over in France. It was in the newspapers. Everyone back home thought the story was true. It was nonsense.'

Twentieth-century literature being his speciality, he no doubt meant that the story was silly – ill-conceived and poorly written – not implausible. But maybe that too. I had only a vague idea of what 'in the newspapers', 'chased by the Germans' and 'everyone back home' meant, and why an angel should be 'daft'.

He told me how my grandfather's detachment had become fragmented on a smallholding at the southern edge of Frameries. I now realise that his account was taken from official citations and from a curious letter written to my grandmother by a second-lieutenant in my grandfather's unit, who saw what happened. Pinned down by a German machine-gun team they'd forced into a barn, my father and a group of his men were working out how to disable it. Without warning, my grandfather dashed to the side of the barn unseen. He tossed something into the entrance over the heads of the machine-gunners. Startled by the noise, they looked behind them as my grandfather entered the barn with his fixed-bayonet rifle, shot dead first the gunner then one of his two comrades and injured the third before they could grab their weapons. This wounded soldier, fumbling with his bayonet, escaped through the back of the building and on to a mound between the barn and the road out of the place. This is where the description took on an unworldly character. The letter-writer, Frank Rochester, with a purplish turn-of-phrase, explained:

*The adversary's rifle must have jammed; but instead of taking a second shot, Horace, your husband, clambered up the slope and faced his mortal enemy. There they stood, steel to glinting steel, like legendary giants atop the globe, having agreed on their choice of weapon and procedure. It seemed like an eternity, that jousting, those lunges and parries, before the foe dropped to his knees and your husband administered the coup de grâce, purposefully and ecstatically downwards from his elevated position of power and authority.*

I can't think how my grandmother responded to that. What did Rochester mean by 'ecstatically'?

But what more can I say? What more have I learned? That valour, if not recklessness, involves the belief that one is being protected by some unseen force?

My grandfather lived to be 96, seemingly indestructible and owing his longevity to some hidden strength. His wife, my grandmother, ever in his shadow and a stranger to the unconventional, died ten years short of their diamond wedding anniversary. On the fiftieth commemoration of the Battle of Mons, the local newspaper ran a story about him. When asked what his secret of survival was, he said nothing but was reported to have had 'a twinkle in his eye'.

What else? In 1921, Second-lieutenant Frank Rochester published a volume of lurid verse under the influence of Aleistair Crowley and then was heard of no more. I'd long thought that something strange was going on. Rochester – he appeared to be a pal (*'Horace, your husband'*) as well as a military subordinate of my grandfather. And Crowley – wasn't he a sinister cove?

That phone call from the undertaker, or mortician, was a summons to my father. According to my mother, he was still muttering when he drove to the funeral parlour. (The breathalyser had been around for twenty years: he wouldn't have passed a test.). My mother's objections were, as always, unavailing. I got the story of those Saturday afternoon events much later, in a phone call from her. She especially remembered the undertaker's expression, 'I'm with him now', which my father had repeated to her, probably as part of some joke suggesting that my grandfather had sprung back into life. The women in my family seem almost seraphic compared with the men and innocent of their subterfuges and roguery. On his return, my father told her nothing. 'Just another bloody formality,' he said, and disappeared to the mini-brewery in his shed.

On his deathbed, my father vouchsafed a lot. He struck me as a prodigal embarked on a late and manic shedding of his record of misconduct, most of it appearing to have been venial. It didn't stop. I visualised him ultimately naked, standing with his modesty covered, a pile of cast-off clothes at his feet. It was then that he said some related thing, as if he'd connected with my image of his absolute divestment and was awaiting exorcism or punishment, the final stage.

'Your grandfather,' he said, and paused.

I almost looked around to see if the ghost of Captain Horace Lennox had entered our hospital side ward where, I guessed, the whizzing but silent throng of doctors and nurses in the corridor had left my father to die in peace. He had his own morphine pump, which he held like a TV zapper; it meant that he would never need to suffer pain again.

'What about him?'

He turned to me, scrambling for the trail of what he'd just said.

'The mark. He showed me. The funeral director. Your grandfather, lying there dead.'

Well, well; even 'mortician' had gone.

'What mark?'

He faced me with a look seemingly aimed at anticipating any disbelief. I'd already raced back to that Saturday afternoon.

'Hare's foot. Foot of a hare. On the inside of his thigh. The mark...'

Before I could get him to explain further, he'd dropped off again, and within two hours he was dead.

I don't know why, but for a while all I could think of was the persistent rumour a few years before that the undertaker's son had been involved in unspeakable acts. I don't know if the undertaker himself, in his phone call that day, was warning my father of something, or seeking enlightenment; or, winking like that general, to establish some kind of brotherhood status. Who has ever seen the foot print of a hare? Would it be something like a cat's but longer? Maybe the undertaker had been stumped and had sought explanation in a book or the advice of a physician friend.

And maybe not. Maybe he knew exactly what it was and was wondering if my father knew too. By such means, one supposes, does the fraternity of evil expand and flourish, even risking the possibility of suspicion being raised if no connection were made. So he'd spotted a hare's footprint on my dead grandfather's body. So what? Why would he have summoned my father to witness it before the mortician's arcane procedures had begun?

Well, the hare's foot is said to be the imprint of the Devil. Someone more fanciful than I might ascribe to it a succession of human flaws in our family; or a line of wickedness that had arbitrarily taken in a Great War general, a decadent minor poet, and my grandfather, who had been winked at by that same commander and whose duel to the death with a German gunner, in his chum Rochester's account, often appears to me as some cosmic battle of wills viewed in slow motion – a battle, of course, in which the designation of the combatants as English and German must be irrelevant and simply illustrative of the paradox of Evil triumphing over Good.

And what of me and my father? Are our peccadilloes but clinging drifts of snow unseen as the thaw continues? And will they manifest themselves in others when the nights draw in again and cold winds begin funnelling from the north below the prickly stars?

Even if I dismiss all this as baloney, my struggle between reason and emotion still lodges in the mind as that epic encounter viewed through the wrong end of a telescope.

For sure, I often dream of me and my grandfather alone and high above clouds of mist on that bridge. He creeps up behind me, lifts me by my armpits, steps closer to the edge, and... well, I don't know what: except that I awake from some free-floating journey beyond his receding form and his echoing belly-laugh.

# COTTONOPOLIS

The Spectre of Grizely. I come and go, come and go...

Yes, I saw enough trouble. I saw misery in the faces of others, especially the young. Some were barely eight years old. Blenkinsop called me 'Mr Shepherd', because I looked after them as best I could. It wasn't my name nor was their custody my official concern: I was about to go away to study and my father thought a stint at Grizely Mill would be an experience. Blenkinsop had me doing all sorts, and told me to take charge of the little ones. They tended to wander, you see, midst the incessant din of the looms; so it became my task to bring them back to their work and stop them straying. 'Mr Shepherd', Blenkinsop would mumble with a grin by way of salutation as he passed me on his rounds. We were told he'd met Arkwright himself: Richard Arkwright, creator by extension of our infernal, dawn-to-dusk racket. I often thought the jangle and clatter of the machines represented wood in protest at its cleaving from the forest, just as the families nigh around and far away were rent asunder to provide us with our begrimed infants.

Blenkinsop definitely knew what was going on with Matthew Witheyshaw. I'd had my eye on Witheyshaw from the beginning, ever since he'd taken personal charge of the Tissington line on my first day; it was our most efficient unit and was operated, it need hardly have been said, by women, mostly of tender years. Many times I watched him stroll up and down behind them and linger now and then to say something in their ears. It was necessary, you understand, to bend close, such was the volume of our all-enveloping tumult, so that instructions could be given and information gained. But Witheyshaw didn't need to stand cheek by jowl – his jowl, their cheek – and cause, by dint of his concealed and short-lived thrusts (well, not hidden from me) those sudden movements, and those looks of mostly pain and revulsion, but sometimes delight, on the women's faces. Also, I frequently saw Blenkinsop, Witheyshaw and the mill hand Worrel talking together like a trio of chin-scratching plotters. Sometimes they would look my way. Perhaps they were discussing me.

One of my duties was to tell the children what Blenkinsop amusingly called 'a scare story'. It concerned a building alongside the huge bale shed. This building was always kept bolted and padlocked, but Blenkinsop, Witheyshaw, and probably Worrel, had access. There were no windows. I had to say that it was haunted, not a word I actually used before those sniffling mites, and that to play near it – not that they had much time for games outside – would result in punishment. He meant birching; it happened in respect of other offences – out of sight and in defiance of rules half-heartedly enforced by those who owned the land on which Grizely and others like it stood, and often the mills themselves. I heard the cries, and ministered to the weals with company goose grease. As I walked the lanes at night, the country piles of those people appeared as illumined ships inviolable on a moonlit ocean, ever drifting away from the sites of their manufactures, called by Mr William Blake 'Satanic', with much justification.

The night, the metaphoric night, closed in. Word spread that Witheyshaw, by dim lamp and in the dust and racket of our unceasing output, had effected congress with one Mildred (Millie) Harrison, whom I'd heard Worrel speak of as 'the Divil's daughter'. This was two days after the disappearance of the Fletcher twins, whom I thought might have fled in terror after I told them to keep away from the building next to the bale shed on account of the bogeymen who waited inside to snatch them from their loved ones (not that many of my listless flock were loved, or had been loved, or ever would be). A few of them went missing; some living locally had simply run back to their families, no doubt for what Blenkinsop described as 'a walloping', and returned after a few days. Others, with the family home the last place they wanted to return to, simply vanished, never to be seen again; one could only hope that they still lived, but what kind of life I dreaded to contemplate. I did all I could to find these absconders, without much success.

For every mudlark lost to us, more arrived. It was as though the coming issue of Millie Harrison, boy or girl, and its crude provenance in the loins of Matthew Witheyshaw happened as part of some agency bound up with the transformation of the contents of those bales into the never-ending extrusion of thread and, in its turn, the absorption of such thread in the myriad weave of cloth, like an endless trail of prodigals consumed by Mr Blake's multi-patterned city.

Checking the stalls one weekend – Blenkinsop was always finding work for me even when the mill was deserted – I picked up a fingertip, its nail cracked and lined with dirt. That I stopped to consider what to do with it meant, I later realised, that I was not yet beyond salvation, that as long as what was wrong with Grizely still kept me awake at night my soul would remain uncorrupted by apathy and lack of concern. I wrapped the fingertip in a wad of oiled rag and took it home, the next day making inquiries on the Tissington line about anyone who had recently suffered a mishap. I might have expected the laughter I aroused as injury after injury was shown to me, Millie Harrison's neighbour revealing a lump on her elbow so shiningly tumescent as to make me wonder how she had continued to work. No doubt Witheyshaw had witnessed my questioning the women, for I saw him talking to them later, all of them looking my way.

I helped in Grizely's accounts office, away from the site of its industry, its steaming cacophony. My work wasn't essential, which was why Blenkinsop extended my responsibilities on a whim. But after the fingertip incident I noticed an increase in his enthusiasm to keep me occupied in any way practical, as my father had wished. Word had got around. I spent more and more time checking invoices and memoranda that didn't need checking. Once, when I stepped out of the office to deal with a boy who seemed to have entered a trance, Witheyshaw appeared as if from nowhere and, with the help of one of the women, led the victim away, looking at me askance. Some evenings, when the children were asleep in their bunkhouse, I would pretend to be checking bills of lading against information in the ledgers. Blenkinsop gave me free run among documentation he barely understood. I was really following the children's trails from their origins in obscurity. The Fletcher boys, like many others, had been brought up North by mail coach from London in freezing weather. Sanctioned by the Guardians of the Poor in Stepney to work at Grizely and other places, they would aid the women at the looms, often being more hindrance than help. I came across a little green book on which was scribbled the title 'Absentia'. I knew what it meant but not why it should appear on a notebook in a place like ours. There, on the first page – clearly a continuation of other 'Absentiae' I couldn't find (themselves having gone missing!) – was a list of ten names with dates in the year of our Lord. At the bottom was the following entry: 'FLETCHER, S. Feb 3 – March 16; FLETCHER, W. Feb 3 – March 16. Sammy and William, the Fletcher twins, not seen since the sixth day of that month. Outside the room I could hear the vestigial hiss of the looms and their after-spasms. Then a floorboard groaned behind me and I turned to see in the doorway the menacing figure of Worrel, bare to the waist and drying himself with a length of filthy towelling. He looked as I had imagined him, a perverted demigod arisen from his watery abode, both mute now and dark with mystery and foreboding.

The following evening, when all was quiet, I returned to Grizely, my parents having smiled at each other as I left on one of my 'romantic' night walks, as the coming terminology had it. Little did they know that my time as supernumerary at the mill was at an end – I'd made the decision – or that under my great coat I carried a jemmy. Having reached the mill, I saw the bunkhouse custodian asleep in her room, her breasts unfettered and two empty quarts of porter telling a tale on the floor beside the bed.

I crossed the yard and approached the door of the forbidden building. I was surprised to see the bolt drawn and the padlock hanging loose. I pushed the door, which resisted pressure, being evidently fastened from inside. I heard what sounded like a commotion behind it and the stifled cry of a child, a boy. Then the door was opened abruptly to reveal a weakly lamp-lit scene. It was Blenkinsop who stood before me, braces hanging down beside his breeches and his vest awry. In the background, not far away, I could see Witheyshaw, who was stood naked. I was sure of that – he was wearing not a stitch; and in front of him, facing me, was the boy, whom Witheyshaw was restraining with his uncouth hands on the lad's shoulders. I may have imagined this, but I saw a second child, or a blurred image of same, escaping into a backdrop of cotton bales, evidently an overflow from the main store or else, and more likely, arranged there as a hiding-place by those damnable servants of Lucifer. Both boys' heads were shaven. I was about to strike out at Blenkinsop when, behind me, as in a sudden rush of air, the figure of Worrel appeared, a cudgel held high in his right hand...

...Years passed in which I tried to put a face to the young victims of that savage debauchery. Was it the Fletcher twins I'd seen, one held fast, his sibling making futile escape into fastnesses from which there could be none? Which was disposed of first, I wondered, Sammy or William; which was the tenth to disappear utterly from their Grizely hell in that year of my sojourn there? It seemed appropriate that in a place defined by figures of the kind I'd pored over – tonnage in, tonnage out, profit and loss, casualties per shift, emoluments made, truck-shop tokens distributed, pounds saved, women and children hired and discharged – those who had flown into the ether, never to be seen again, should be numbered, their nominal state finally robbing them of what little humanity they possessed on arrival. But memory comes and goes, mostly goes.

*

What was all the foregoing? I know not but have inklings.

After a while, as of time spent in Purgatory, I came, have come, to terms with the world, to fill the dank air here with myself *in extenso* and beyond; insensate, without will, and lacking human predicate, so that I simply am and have been – unencumbered with thoughts of *Why?* or *When?* I see without evaluating what passes before me, without the desideratum of function, deprived of all interventionary impulse, destitute of curiosity. I observe without comment, journey without destination, alight without regret, sometimes seen – a wraith – sometimes not. The world is at is whenever and wherever it is; it is, was, and ever more shall be. I am a miasma of particles, a cloud of midges mad above the pond at twilight, a sky-filled swarm of starlings playing a game of *Shapes* in silent and wondrous murmuration and communing. Then I became apparition, spirit; a presence, an absence. What I knew, I was forgetting, am forgetting, will forget.

For the moment, though, I inhabit this derelict building, this shell. Crows explode from its hollow windows like shrapnel from the battlefields of Blenheim, Ramillies, Oudenarde. (What are these places, these conflicts? From my studies?) They come here now, the visitors, in their crinoline and tweeds to bear some sort of witness. One is borne aloft on disparate wheels conjoined, which suggests the words penny and farthing, but what these are I am unaware. The visitants are down there on the towpath, seemingly shivering with expectation. They point. 'Do you see him?' they exclaim. 'Look! There. Up there.' But I am gone, leaving them in doubt but with a story for any open-mouthed auditor back home; and I am suddenly hovering at night in a vernal wood I know not where. It is the same place I am being brought back to again and again. Here are shadowy figures carrying sacks over their shoulders. Here are those same creatures digging in the loam and burying their burdens; here they are, laughing and spitting and joking, and making light. Then they go, are going, have gone, leaving me sentinel above the plot they've camouflaged.

The wood grows quiet. Nothing stirs. But, infused among the trees, I rustle their leaves in anger, unseen, and I know not why; and then I repair in perturbation of spirit to my place in the window beyond the excursions of the curious, beyond the ruckus and uproar I remember.

# INCIDENT AT THE LOCH

At school we had an English teacher called Punch Evans, who it was said had been some kind of Army boxing champion. We never went into the details – you simply didn't – though it must have occurred to us that he would have joined the Forces through choice: by that time, there'd been no National Service for about twenty years. The few who questioned him about it were given minimising short shrift. Other things had changed. Punch was one of the few on the staff to wear a graduate's gown in class. It was too big for him, or he'd somehow made himself look smaller, because it kept slipping from his shoulders and he would have to yank it back. He spent a lot of time at the blackboard, writing down lines of poetry, snatches of dialogue from plays, and expressions such as 'negative capability' – and tugging at his gown; he would then turn to face us, each time seeming to do so like a man confronting an accuser. His nose was misshapen, so perhaps that was it: he'd spent ages shielding himself as best he could from public gaze, and this was how he'd at last surmounted his embarrassment. It was a decisive moment, slow and deliberate and endlessly repeated.

Once we'd reached the sixth form, Punch started calling us by our first names ('Christian', then; that's changed too).

There were eleven of us doing English. Our first term was heavy with dank leaf fall and rainy evenings, as if reminders of the gravity of what we'd undertaken, or of mists and mellow fruitfulness. Our set texts were mountainous in their challenge if not in their height as a pile of books, though that was impressive enough when it included Punch's suggestions for extra reading.

On the first day of A-level, by way of introduction, Punch announced that he was a Tolstoyan.

'Anyone know what I mean?' he asked. 'Not you, Roberts.'

We sniggered, Punch smiled. Mike Roberts was related to Punch, some kind of cousin once removed – far enough, anyway, to make them virtually strangers to each other. We all knew, and Punch knew that we knew. But Mike had little to say about his relative, perhaps as a result of some tacit agreement between them. Punch rarely called on Mike by name, first or other. When he required a response from one of us and Mike raised his hand – in truth, the arm speared upwards like a Nazi salute had, in our graduation to the sixth, reduced to a waving finger – he would just nod once in Mike's direction, his raised eyebrows beckoning an answer. It was probably a conscious move: Mike was by far the brightest among us, later the head boy with a place at Cambridge, and already a contributor of essays to the school magazine. If anyone had known what 'Tolstoyan' meant, it would have been Mike. Anyway, the best we others could come up with was the ironically facetious 'Someone who likes the works of Tolstoy?' Mike and Punch grinned at each other. Before Mike could reply with a similar interrogative lift to indicate that he might not be correct – though clever, he was modesty personified – Punch told us himself: 'My attitude to art is moral'. By art, of course, he meant English literature. Freddie Wilson, the joker in our pack and destined to work on the *Daily Mirror*, said he hadn't realised Tolstoy was English. (In truth, many of our answers to questions like this were half-jocular, including the one about Tolstoy's admirers. We were thought of as 'clever'.)

All of us were studying a couple of other subjects, but the teachers for them encouraged few extra-curricular activities. Punch did. During those two years, he organised something once a term: theatre visits, 'pilgrimages' to places enshrined in books – Wordsworth's Tintern was one – and days out at literary festivals. English was not just study for examinations, though that too: it was what he called ' a preparation for life': not an original view, the widely-read Mike confided, quoting F. R Leavis or someone similar.

In summer, Punch invited us all to the house where he lived with his elderly father. It happened twice – initially at the end of our first year, the second time twelve months later before our exam results were due. He'd been at the school for only three years and we were the first of his A-level pupils ('students' now) to be accorded the privilege.

Their house stood on its own in our impoverished Valleys town more notable for its serpentine terraces, which struggled up hills before skedaddling down the other side. It was called The Manse. In its way it was a throwback to a time of much wider poverty, when as a symbol of its occupant's high social rank it loomed much larger. Half its encircling trees had been felled. By our time, according to Punch, it had become part of 'Snobs Row', though the locals, perhaps knowing the reduced circumstances of those who once lived there, never made an issue of it. The father, in any case, had been a coalminer, like a lot of other older men in the town. In the fireplace was a Davy Lamp sculpted from a huge chunk of coal, presented to him by his collier pals when he retired. We assumed that funds for the house had been inherited from the mother, whoever she'd been. Mike had told us she was dead. There were photographs of her on the sideboard, a refined-looking woman, almost a beauty, and with half a knowing smile, as though a second after the photograph was taken she had erupted with laughter. There was a picture of a young boy and girl too, Punch and his sister.

Freddie Wilson, Mike and I got on well together. We were the 'scholarship' trio. Mike's breadth of knowledge and Freddie's wit sought each other out, to the extent that Mike divulged to Freddie more from what little he knew about Punch than we knew from him or from Punch directly. This, for some reason, only happened during our final term, especially in those weeks after our exams were over and before we finished school for good. In those days and at our school, we had no time off, and it was spent with Punch discussing the wider implications of the books we'd studied.

On that last summer day at The Manse the whole class – our trio and eight others – were invited. Punch and his father had supplied what used to be called 'strong drink' – bottles of beer and cider – suspecting quite rightly that we were well used to its taste. Punch had arranged a fish 'n' chips supper for us all. Freddie, sitting cross-legged in a chair opposite Punch, casually took a cigarette from a metal case, tapped the business end on the lid, and lit up with a Zippo, only offering the re-opened case to Punch and his father after doing so. Both declined.

'Does our Michael smoke?' the old man asked, the 'our' seeming to suggest the familial connection, a reduction of distance, rarely before acknowledged.

'Mike's a paragon,' Freddie said, and, with a glance at Punch: 'That's true, isn't it, Mr Evans?'

Punch didn't know what to say, and just shrugged his shoulders.

'You see, Mr Evans,' Freddie continued, addressing the older man this time, 'your son has taught us to live by the book. Or should I say "books"? If a book doesn't teach us a lesson, a lesson to live by, it ain't much cop. Mike believes in all that stuff. Frankly, to me it makes every book seem like the Holy Bible.'

The old man just nodded, maybe not understanding, amused or confused perhaps by the way Freddie's final sentences had slipped into the idiomatic, and Punch looked embarrassed at his father's ignorance. The other boys were outside on the patio, beyond an open French window whose net curtains billowed now and then, the signal of what would soon be a change in the weather. Once or twice, bottles in hand, they would fall silent and look into the room, seeking proof among those sitting inside of an opinion one of them had expressed, a controversial one maybe, now unfettered by classroom constraints and decorum, by a life once disciplined but now floating freely in the interregnum between school and university, adolescence and adulthood.

When it was time to eat, Mike laid the long kitchen table while Punch and I drove in his car to town for the food, the individual orders falling into four separate batches. A few of the others got in the back just for the ride. Punch told me it was lucky there was a big table; it had been included in the house sale with a few other sticks of furniture. I was about to say that it was a huge house for three people but stopped myself because I was assuming that Punch had been an only child. A mistaken assumption, as it turned out.

By the time we got back, it was raining heavily under low cloud. Punch's father was sitting in the middle of the settee, with Mike and Freddie seeming to bear down on him on either side. He'd already switched the oven on to warm up the food. Old man Evans, who looked more of a pugilist than his son, was explaining something, to judge by Mike's and Freddie's intent looks. The others, those who'd stayed behind, were in separate groups, having their own conversations. I caught the end of what Evans senior was telling Mike and Freddie:

'After that we didn't see much of Tony or his folks. I don't know why. It wasn't our fault.'

Freddie and Mike were each clutching a bottle of lager. There were six empty bottles on the coffee table in front of them. Punch's father had been drinking too.

'Come and get it!' Punch called out, as a few of us slid the fish and chips on to plates.

Punch's father stood up, unsteady on his feet.

'You OK, Pop?' Punch asked.

His father gave a comic salute with his forefinger and hobbled towards the kitchen. We'd already been there for two hours and had drunk a fair amount, coaxed by bravado. Well, our school days were over.

We were half way through our meal when I asked: 'Who was Tony?'

It was what we all did, what Punch had encouraged us to do: ask questions, get the information flowing, draw conclusions, make up our own minds – about T S Eliot and stuff.

Mike answered: 'Mr Evans's school pal. They were all on a camping holiday in Scotland. Isn't that right, Mr Evans?' Was Mike's formality deliberately increasing the gap between himself and those distant relatives? A few of us glanced from one to another. Drink had confused the Evanses in our understanding.

'That's right,' the old man said. 'Got into a bit of a scrape did Tony and Richard here.'

Richard 'Punch' Evans. We knew his real name, of course. But the informality with which Punch had ushered in the two years of A-level by calling us by our first names had not applied to our dealings with him. He was not

Richard; he was still Punch, though we never used that name in front of him either; he was Mr Evans, or Sir. I think he quietly balked at the last as a remnant of a lower-school deference he now considered irrelevant. He knew his nickname, of course; the other members of staff probably knew theirs too.

You could almost sense what was imminent, that someone from among those who'd only eavesdropped on Mike, Freddie and Punch's father ten minutes before, would ask the question. I forget who it was.

'Scrape?'

Our heads were down, our knives and forks clashing with crockery, and bottles were being emptied, our guzzling heads thrown back. The word seemed to creep to the centre of the table unnoticed, rise a couple of feet and hang there, its question mark flashing.

Old Mr Evans was only too willing to explain: 'Margaret had died, see. Hole in the heart. We never knew. You didn't then. We had to get away, to forget. Well, not to forget, but you know what I mean. Richard here took it bad, even though he was sixteen. We all did. We went camping by a loch. Scotland. Richard was pally with Anthony – Tony – so he came along too. Didn't he, Richard?'

All heads except old Mr Evans's turned towards Punch for an explanation of this telegraphese.

'Margaret was my thirteen-year-old sister,' Punch explained. 'She had atrial septal defect, or ASD.'

He sounded as though he were apologising to us boys for the ugly expression, 'hole in the heart', and his father's statement that he had taken his sister's death 'bad'.

But the father, seemingly indignant at the son's trumping of his description with this technical term, butted in, his voice thinly coated with censure:

'Richard and Tony went off to explore. An hour later, along comes Tony running towards us. His face was white as a sheet. Hobbling behind him about fifty yards away was Richard here with his face covered in blood. His hands were over his face like as if his head was going to fall off, isn't it? Never seen so much blood on a young 'un. Tony was shaking. He told us they'd been attacked, by some gang or other. Glasgow yobs.'

Punch swiped his nose with the ball of his thumb. Was it a signal to make the connection between the incident and what we'd thought was the result of successive batterings in the ring? Would a champion have taken much of a beating?

With his comment on this, one of the others made things worse, as it were:

'Tell us about boxing for the Army, Punch.'

We all stared at each other. None of us had ever called him Punch in his presence. It was drink unlocking doors. Nor had we questioned him, as I said, about the Forces or his sporting prowess, any more than we'd have asked 'Drag' Denison, the French master, how he'd come by his limp, s*a boiterie.*

Punch was about to speak when his father jumped in first. 'Richard was never in the Army, never been a soldier,' he said. 'Where did you get that? And boxing? You must be daft, the lot of you. Books was all he was interested in.' Like you bunch, he might have added.

There was an edge to his voice, an all-embracing censure or contempt aimed at his son as much as at us, this crowd of smart Alecs who'd invaded his privacy Later, much later, we'd see this as Mike expressed it when he referred to education as 'the Great Divider'. He meant the gulf that learning, books, opened up between us and people like Punch's father.

'Yes – where did you get that idea?' Punch asked. It was hard to believe he hadn't known. He wasn't drinking much, we noticed.

We all shrugged, sensing the need to avoid spoiling our evening. But it was too late, the downpour and early darkness outside seeing to that. We could hear the rain drumming on something metallic beyond the window, some lid or roof. Though we'd finished eating, neither Punch nor his father made any attempt to return to the siting-room. We'd all stopped drinking too; we'd had enough, and we had to get home, those of us being picked up not wanting to embarrass our parents or whoever it was had arranged to drive there. Some of us lived close enough at a stretch to walk, but we didn't want to stagger. It was an exaggeration to say that Punch wasn't drinking much: he'd drunk hardly anything. There'd been this sequence: outdoor (patio), front room (as we called it in that place), kitchen, later front room as departure lounge.

Evans senior opened another bottle, his sixth or seventh. Its cap bounced on the tiled floor. He was beyond offering us more as the perfect host, or the perfect host's helper; we could please ourselves. Mike tried to change the subject by mentioning an upcoming TV documentary about Seamus Heaney, which he said would include a criticism of the poet by someone called Paul Danziger. Mike must have seen the look of disdain on the face of Evans senior, who may not have heard of Heaney, let alone Paul Danziger. (Actually, none of us at that moment had heard of Danziger, and that might have included Punch: Mike was avenues ahead of us all.)

Although it was early summer, we could have done with the lights on. Punch nor his father made the move. The father had more to say about that Highlands episode, something about the police confirming the culprits were Glaswegian but not doing anything, as if dragging it back to the table after he'd seen it tip-toeing away and looking over the shoulder at us in case of needing to make a bolt for it.

'I didn't take to Tony – Anthony,' he said, uttering the longer form of the name with what sounded like scorn. 'Margaret didn't too, the wife neither.' An emboldened Freddie might have asked at that juncture if Punch's mother didn't have a name, or why, despite the family's dislike of Richard's pal, they'd gone camping to Scotland. And what was a woman with enough money to buy an Edwardian pile doing marrying a coalminer? We all seemed captive, Punch as well, himself perhaps wanting something to be said as the last word. He placed his knife and fork on the plate in the position of twenty past four; his father's remained where they had been set either side of the table mat. Go on, Punch appeared to be saying. Get on with it if you're going to.

'We never found out why that bunch of Jocks did it – did we, Richard? This said without looking at his son.

'No, we didn't,' Punch confirmed, still self-absorbed, head lowered. 'It was unprovoked.'

'Aye,' his father said. 'No reason for it whatever.'

After the washing-up, we finally strayed into the sitting-room. Evans senior had taken up position in front of the TV. There was some quiz show on; we'd heard its low-volume antiphonies of laughter and applause while the last plates were being dried and put away, but now they were louder. The old man had turned the sound up when he realised we were all returning. He'd also pulled his chair closer to the screen, his head craned forwards into its phosphorescent exclusion zone. He'd done with conversation. We could look at him more closely and relate his peculiarities to the bits and bobs in the room, to the huge room itself even, lit only by the TV's buzzing source of illumination. It silvered the photograph frames and their commemorations: Mrs Evans, about to chuckle at whatever had taken her fancy; sickly Margaret, not knowing how close the end was; and Margaret and Punch, the siblings together with all to live for. Punch did nothing to suggest that his father had not drawn the evening to a close. It was all a bit embarrassing. Draped across chairs or spread out on the floor, we looked at each other and exchanged small talk. Mike, recalling the evening a few years afterwards, said it had reminded him of of two communities, with Punch 'shadowed' in the doorway and maybe hoping – though he must have been confident of our success – that we'd be moving away from the life his father had led, further than he had anyway. Mike had seen what we'd seen: a retired coalminer made faintly embittered, even angry, by consumption of alcohol that now served only to reveal his reduced capacity and what Mike referred to, unfairly in my view, as the 'qualitative' difference between us. Being charitable might have led us to think that he'd meant 'quality of life'. We seemed to be putting the worst complexion on things: that miner's lamp made from coal, for example, a symbol of a life petrified in its element.

The Manse commanded heights before the land behind heaved itself upwards just once more towards dripping afforestation and spoil tips. We never wondered why the trees surrounding it had been chopped down or why their ugly stumps had been left in the ground for so long – to rot away, perhaps. A drive led to one of the top roads and its light traffic. The valley bottom could be seen much further down, its orange street lamps strung out and blinking through sheets of rain and premature darkness. It would be ever thus: 'No escape from geography apart from anything else,' Freddie once said.

My older brother picked us up in his car – me, Mike, and Freddie. As we drove away, I could see Punch silhouetted in an upstairs window, staring out at us, at the world, and below him the sitting-room window and its flickering TV semaphore.

'A hole in the heart,' Mike said, once we were on our way. 'I swear I never knew.'

'And that Caledonian caper,' Freddie said, after a pause for reflection. 'What the fuck was that all about?'

# BLOGPOST FROM AN OLDER WOMAN

Well, that's everything done. All packed.

I'm looking again at the card they've sent this time, with a personalised note written in gold ink, as if with a Midas fountain pen. Do they know something I don't? After the second visit, they have always posted me a welcome two weeks before my arrival, because I always book. (It appears on standard black business cards marked, Fernsby Island Hotel. S.J. Holmes, Assistant Manager.) Customer care, I've assumed. But never before in gold, or with a personal addendum. Funny.

Educated woman of a certain age, I suppose they think of me behind my back, a lady poised between elegance and fading allure, with gentility a guarantee of protection, especially against gentlemen of a certain age, the worst sort. I sometimes recognise myself in fictional characters, which is why I read selected women novelists, fascinated by how close they might come to describing me in detail. It's never happened, probably because we never really compare with the complexities of invented people, who need to abide by an ever-unravelling plot. But I dare say I'm not without interest: a short story, maybe, rather than a novel.

It's as a woman cheerfully unescorted that I wish to see myself. A widow, yes; then a divorcée, yes. But no-one in tow and no-one, as it were, towing me; and never having either to raise a question or elicit a smirk. I've never needed anyone to take the place of those I've lost, either by death or bad behaviour. It's a test of my independence and my ability to rise above the low expectations of others. But not everyone: things get better, matters improve. In an age when having a door held open for you by a male – it's always a man – can give the old and simple idea of chivalry a sinister twist or, not having it done, indicate failing standards of decorum, you have to make quick judgements.

David, 'Biblical David' as I used to call him, wouldn't have had anything to do with this glistering card of welcome. I met him there last time, doing the same as me apparently: a man at a table for one a few yards over from a woman at a table for one, each pondering a single fresh carnation in separate long-necked vases. He claimed not to have known that for three years I'd been spending a week there in June. When he reminded me that it was where we'd sometimes thought of staying together, it was possible that his arrival was nothing more than chance. I didn't need reminding. The amusing thing was that they couldn't immediately replace our two single tables with a table for two. Odd for an establishment that could run to gilded cards of welcome, I know, but it took them twenty-four hours to re-arrange things, mainly because I didn't straight away want them re-arranged. Not that David and I didn't speak while we were there, but for the first dinner we each sat alone, trying not to catch each other's attention yet indulging in meaningful stares. At the end of that week, having avoided talking about our past together and ignored each other for long periods, except to mention mutual friends and what they'd been up to, we both left on the quaint contraption they use to reach the mainland three hundred yards away at low tide, though not at the same time. We just said it had been good to see each other again, which was a half-truth. But that was it. No farewell kisses. We'd behaved as though we were strangers newly met, with all that meant for me in my determination not to collapse in a romantic heap of regret and nostalgia. As I got into my car I could see him on the landing stage with a few other guests waiting for the return of the four-wheeled buggy, his raincoat folded over a suitcase. He was talking to a woman we'd met, a married woman waiting for her husband. Good, I thought.

I don't expect to see David there this year. We haven't communicated in the past twelve months, but I possibly made a mistake in telling him that my presence there had become an annual event. I didn't intend refusing to go just because he might decide to make a surprise appearance again. Of course, he might turn up for the same disinterested reason that I shall.

David was not the same as Will. When Will died on me – literally, I like to joke to myself, though everyone must have put two and two together from what I'd said – David was there to help. But we've all grown up to understand that a man's help and support entertains the possibility of ambivalence. I wonder if men in my position feel the same way? Somehow, I think not. It must be every man's dream to feel that he will soon submit to a woman's sexual advances, especially if they catch him off guard or unprepared, so for him a relationship is assumed to hold that early possibility of congress, even if it never materialises. Will was the one who misbehaved; he was the misbehaving widow-maker, whereas David's lack of transgression was almost Christian, hence my nickname for him. Funnily enough, I used to hate him for it, particularly as it was my misconduct that led to the divorce. I wish he'd misbehaved more, though we were too old to establish openness after the event – or events; that has to be done at the outset before either party has committed anything, and even then it might founder in a collapse of good intentions, as it did with my friends Millie and Ken. I haven't seen either of them for ages, but we phone now and again and send Christmas cards. Neither Millie nor I managed to bring children into the world.

Just as I was about to drive away last time, Steve Holmes – 'S.J. Holmes, Assistant Manager' – was arriving for his afternoon shift. The weather had changed, and it was spitting rain. I could see his car creeping towards me as my windscreen wiper sluiced away a week's gritty splodges. He pulled in beside me against the wall, in that old Triumph Herald of his. He's a classic-car enthusiast, as he once told me (I don't know how that cropped up in conversation). The Triumph reminded me of how Marjorie's mum used to look: an ancient buffed to a super-shine that surely outmatched her inner workings, though like Steve's ministerings to the Triumph's moving parts, she kept

139

herself fit and healthy. I suppose Steve is thirty or more years my junior, but we talk as coevals, if that isn't too presumptuous on my part. AInstAM, the proverbial 'letters' after his name, stands for Associate of the Institute of Administrative Management. I'm old enough to be his mother, as they say of women suspected of unseemly acts.

One afternoon, while walking on the island path close to the rocks, I looked down and saw Steve in a swimsuit clambering on to the wooden diving platform in the cove. It was as if he'd revealed a part of himself that his duty did not encompass or sanction, a secretive act to which he knew I was privy; I noticed a quick turn of his head my way before the revelation, but no formal acknowledgement of my presence. I could have been wrong. As usual with me in such matters these days, the thought was short-lived and soon forgotten. I remembered that he'd made a perfect entry into the water, leaving a small white circle that soon imploded, like a film run backwards. When he returned to the platform, and before levering himself for another dive, he sort of suspended himself in the water by his elbows, and looked out to sea through a gap in the rocks. In the car park last time, we exchanged small talk, he standing next to my part-opened window and looking in. Then, as the rain became heavier, he ran off to catch the waiting buggy, the one I'd come ashore on. But before dropping down to the jetty, he stopped, turned towards me, and waved. Then, a few months ago, I had a phone text. It was from Steve. It said, 'Hope you don't mind me contacting you. I got your number from the guest info. Thought you might like this.

I've swapped the Herald for it.' Seconds later, a picture popped on to the screen of a green and gleaming Triumph TR3 sports car. I replied, 'Very nice,' and left it at that. I thought about the message a few times but didn't dwell on it. I did send a follow-up a few weeks later: 'Hope the Triumph is still going. I'll be at the Fernsby again this year.' There was no reply.

I often wonder if our best intentions are not undermined by things beyond our control. I look in the wardrobe mirror. Why have I dressed this way? Why these shoes, this blouse, the bolero jacket that always makes me look, well, too young? It's to do with feeling right – but right for what, for whom? For me? And if for me, to what end other than self-satisfaction? Is a woman without escort waiting to be escorted? Is her reluctance to submit to the customary sequence of events when in the company of a man the victory over the tyranny she expects him to exert, or a denial of her own impulses? Every summer at the hotel there are couples. The ones I get to know are married. Some partners barely speak to each other at meal times. One might stare out of the window while the other, looking wistful, re-arranges the sugar cubes in their pot with a dinky silver spoon. Sometimes, though possibly I imagine it, the woman will look my way and smile. I return it not as an acknowledgement of some instinctive but tacit female confederacy, but as an act that two men who were strangers to each other would never countenance: there are sisterhoods but no brotherhoods. Perhaps it would be better if there were. I am returning her recognition of there

141

being some region of mutual interest to us as women, a kind of refuge in times of anguish where we will exchange more than sighs of resignation.

It's just that Steve Holmes' wave on the mainland jetty last time has stayed with me and brought my memories of him into focus. His facial features become clearer. I begin to remember small things about him: the way he skips down the central stairway and takes the final two steps in one neat jump; his diplomatic intervention at table that time after one of the waiters had been unjustly criticised for something by a guest; the time I saw him one evening, on his way home, pushing the Triumph towards the car park's exit, the driver's door open and his left hand on the steering-wheel as he ran faster and faster until he dropped into his seat and the vehicle shot off with a belch of exhaust smoke. He wears suede brogues; sometimes brown, sometimes blue. It's as though I am being handed pieces of a jigsaw, and some force unseen is encouraging me to snap them into place. As a picture nears completion, I see its other elements, things I'd forgotten, such as Clive the odd-job man plucking dusty anthers from the vase of lilies at Reception so that they cannot brush their indelible pollen on passers-by, and the few men on their own who sometimes stay and whom I hitherto remember only as courteous presences, perhaps, like me, not wishing to disturb the tranquillity which others like them, like me, have created to make any advance beyond politeness seem untoward and cheap. Perhaps this world I'm re-creating, one I'd forgotten for a twelvemonth, is revealing a truth that's asking to be confronted: that someone, a man, has noticed something about me that I've hitherto exposed by my vulnerability or shielded with my obstinacy. Both Will and David said I had 'an obstinate streak', like some grey fault line in a head of long black hair.

Anyway, I'm ready to go. I've convinced myself that Steve's final wave on my departure last time was not unthinking formality. The message and picture, too, must have meant something. But I'm not obsessed by it: the gold greetings card may this year have gone to all the other summer visitors too. My re-forming image, however, does not admit that; it finds a place for a young man wishing to make an exception for me and buying a special pen from a craft shop. I have an image of sitting outside with him on his afternoon off – he 'lives in' during the week and goes home at weekends, wherever that is – and being bored to pleasant distraction by talk of valves and piston rings as I re-position a lock of my hair that some quickened breeze has dislodged. In my picture, my slow-moving tableau, David, as I suspected and hoped, has not shown; at least he's not there when I am: I don't go at the same time every year, so his appearance a second time would possibly be coincidence. He moves in a different direction beyond the picture's border; he is a blur beside the palms. Whereas Steve, although trying not to be obvious, is slightly over-attentive towards me and rapidly coming into full focus.

I can believe how some might see my imaginings as the pathetic fantasy of an older woman in thrall to a much younger man, not understanding how, first, there is nothing wrong with that; and, second, that the reverse – a young male having designs on an unsuspecting mature woman, or even a woman of his own generation – is simply what always happens because women allow it to. I am not a standard-bearer; I am following my own inclinations. I'm following my instincts.

I take a last look in the mirror. I'm almost sixty. In thinking I look ten years younger I'm not deluding myself. Others have said so. I've kept my shape, which I contour from the waist in a downward smoothing motion with both hands that is now sensual as well as confirming. I see me lowering myself into my three-year-old Mazda sports, careless of momentarily exposing my thighs and black lace stocking-tops in the inevitable and inelegant tangle of legs, and I lie back, lowered, almost supine, as if in a bed.

It's an eighty-mile journey to the Fernsby, an Art Deco hotel and the only building on the island. Daphne du Maurier stayed there a few times; there's a Lady Browning Suite, with an explanation that she was a Dame and that Browning was her married name. It's horrendously exorbitant. The buggy takes ten minutes to cross the strand at low water, pulled by a Tonka-like vehicle with four huge wheels. We passengers rock back and forth like animals in a travelling menagerie. I've heard the crossing described as 'an expensive inconvenience' – I call it The Fernsby Oxymoron. The owners wanted to build a helipad but couldn't get planning permission. It's a five-star, costly place, although for me the expense buys simplicity.

My jigsaw is almost complete. Next time I see Steve Holmes on the diving platform down in the cove I will linger and he will see me lingering. Other things may have happened before then, to do with my being 'forward', as my mother called it, and his breaches of protocol. But if they don't, it will be no matter. It will all depend on the meaning of a farewell wave and the writing of an advance greeting card by someone with a long memory who has brought a fancy pen to be used just once. There are good omens, as there have always been: David and Will both smile at me in technicolour from their separate frames on my dressing-table, and – you have to take my word for it – my disappointments never last long and have had little effect on the revival of optimism.

But I'm way ahead of myself.

The sun shines. I shall grab my suitcase, lock the front door, and squeeze into the car. There is something – don't you think? – about the sky above the horizon as you are approaching the coast that proclaims the existence of what you desire, what you deserve, albeit momentarily out of sight. My father used to call it the ozone, a layer of burnished light blue below an immensity of sky. As Ms du Maurier once said (and I quote from the Fernsby's brochure), 'Luxury has never appealed to me; I like simple things: books, being alone, or with somebody who understands.'

# KANDULA THE ELEPHANT

A few months after my father died and I'd jokingly referred to me and my sister as orphans in our late forties – our mother had died three years before – I received a strange letter from my Uncle Ralph in Ilfracombe.

Inside the letter was a newspaper cutting and a photograph.

Uncle Ralph was my mother's brother. An amateur photographer and magician, he was a bit odd, the perfect example of how remote one's childless aunts and uncles can be. It's as if only chance has prevented their becoming your parents; they stand apart, a tad aggrieved at some missed opportunity. Sometimes (and this is my curiosity sparking at full voltage) they express a coldness towards their fecund siblings amounting to estrangement. For most of my life, I'd probably met Uncle Ralph no more than six times.

But there may have been an additional reason for his isolation. The letter was written on notepaper belonging to Oakland Vale, Barnstaple; it's a care home, but they don't call it that.

'Childless' is only partly correct. When I was a teenager, my mother showed me a photograph of Ralph and his wife, Vera. On Aunty Vera's lap was their baby boy, wearing a frilly dress and probably a few weeks away from being able to walk. I can't remember what caught my attention first: the grim expressions on the faces of Ralph and Vera or what appeared to be some kind of joke they were playing with the connivance of their little lad, whose name was Gabriel. Ralph and Vera were staring not so much at the photographer – it was a studio shot that included an aspidistra and a backdrop of Elysian fields – as straight and accusingly at the viewer. I looked at Gabriel and then at the ground beneath the trio's feet, for Gabriel's eyes were half-risen suns and looking down with an almost comic astonishment. Vera was supporting Gabriel's head, holding him upright. What was about to happen? Were the parents' earnest features and the son's complicity in something so far unseen all about to erupt in laughter, to be revealed in a subsequent photo that had somehow been lost?

Hardly anyone writes letters these days, not personal ones at least. I was on my mobile when Ralph's arrived. I rang my sister, Miriam. I couldn't tell her everything of what Ralph had written, only that he'd done so in confidence. I'd had a vague memory of where he lived: some nursing home in the West Country. The letter was written in a spectral hand. I imagined Ralph wasn't smiling as he wrote; he would have if the ink had been invisible. It was the kind of ruse he used to perform at Christmas when we were kids. We'd have to light a candle and get my mother and father to hold the letter over the flame. Ralph and Vera always signalled their presence by sending us things in the post.

'What does he want?' Miriam asked.

'I'm not quite sure. That's if he wants anything at all. It's really weird. To be honest, I'm partly shocked.'

She accepted the confidentiality and changed the subject. Miriam and I see a fair bit of each other since what happened between her and her husband. We never sob on each other's shoulders. But loyalty is always there, waiting to be called up.

'Do you remember visiting?' she said. 'You know: on the paddle-steamer?'

I did. Half way across the Channel from its embarkation dock on the Welsh coast, the *P. S. Waverley* ploughed into jade waters, leaving the muddy ones behind in its twin-paddled wake. That was the only time we'd been over there. My father spent most of the voyage below deck, watching the oiled pistons pump with shining, maiden-voyage efficiency, though the previous winter the *Waverley* had completed its third refit. It had done duty in places far away and forgotten.

'We must have been going there for a reason.'

'We were. Don't you remember? Aunty Vera had had a baby.'

'Gabriel.'

'Yes. Gabriel.'

Our exchange was like this because we were reaching for long-buried memories, the sort that reminded you of how much you'd hidden or abandoned, which amounted to the same thing. Our family had developed a rarefied sense of the unspeakable; we were an abstemious lot.

148

Miriam said it first: 'There was something wrong. Wasn't there?'

We knew there was, or we half-knew. An abstemious family values silence as a way of dealing with threats to the unutterable. Memories are allowed to fritter away. In the end, they're all we have.

'Did you know that Gabriel is a virtue name?' Miriam asked.

I didn't. I do now. I Googled it and discovered Patience, Prudence, Chastity. Mostly girls' names.

'I remember mum saying they wanted a girl,' she said.

'I didn't know that. Does wanting and not getting mean disappointment?'

'Probably.'

'So was it an act of commiseration, that Ilfracombe trip?' I was being slightly ridiculous.

'I don't think so. I don't know. I remember the gulls.'

I did too. As the boat sneaked into the harbour, paddles reversed and pistons slowed, the gulls shrieked above us, like portents. There was a climb as soon as we land-lubbered off the ramp – a trudge up hill to where Ralph and Vera lived in a sugar-cube cottage called Rosemergy. In his letter, Ralph had written the name in capitals. It must have been years since he'd lived there. He'd also spelled it ROSMERGY. I somehow twigged it was incorrect.

'Do you know,' Miriam said. 'Now I come to think about it, they knew the way so they must have been there before.'

'Must have. It didn't register with me. Did they know the way? I don't remember.'

'Nor with me till now. Because I'm sure mum told me on the way over that it was only the second time she'd visited her brother since he and Vera had moved to Devon.'

'Why did they move?'

'Because Vera's parents had lived there. I don't know what happened to them. They died, I suppose. She lived near us. Didn't you know? There's a picture, some Sunday School outing.'

I didn't. I remember the photo of a Methodist gathering on the hillside: young people nestled together and smiling with a couple of their elders in collars and ties and Hombergs, despite what was evidently a hot day. Later, it would remind me of some idyllic joy before a catastrophe.

I told Miriam: 'What I do remember is dad walking up the hill in front of us, turning off down a couple of side lanes, and standing with his hand on Rosemergy's wooden gate, waiting for us to catch up. He seemed to know where he was going. Perhaps he'd been given directions.'

'Well, we're orphans now so we can't ask.'

I smiled. 'No,' I said.

Miriam asked if I remembered Ralph's Christmas cards. They were the same every year. By some dark-room sleight of hand, he contrived to set smiling portrait heads of himself and Vera against a wintry Ilfracombe scene on a postcard inside a traditional shop-bought greetings card. Like the best amateur work, they looked almost professional – almost. There was only one of him, Vera, and Gabriel. They were smiling then; but there were several years when they didn't smile, when the seasonal postcards never arrived. They ceased soon after that dour studio portrait with the aspidistra.

'Their cottage,' Miriam said, 'It was so... so doll's house.'

I must have been about ten. When we went through into the front-room my mother and father had to lower their heads in the doorway, and they weren't that tall. Gabriel was lying in a cot with wooden fence-like sidewalls, not making a sound. I wasn't tall enough to reach over the top, so held on to the sidebars and peered through, as though what I was looking at was imprisoned. Gabriel, silent and pink, with the seagulls still screeching outside, was floating on his back in a foam of white wool and satin. It's funny how memories, once concentrated on, begin picking up more detail. The demeanour of Ralph and Vera, for example, when Miriam asked if Gabriel was asleep. He was asleep, Vera said, but he had this way of dozing. She said it as though it were some kind of trick he'd learned from his part-time wizard of a father. I looked closer, my nose between two of the bars. Gabriel's eyelids weren't fully closed. I could see him looking down, staring at something on his chest, maybe the vestige of some dried yellow pap. And there was a smell, a whiff of something. As if disappointed at the unforthcoming sequel to this display, Ralph stepped forward and prodded him lightly on his little shoulder. I'm sure Vera grabbed Ralph's arm and restrained him. Anyhow, Gabriel didn't move, let alone wake. Ralph had prodded poor Gabriel, their baby, an un-cooperative sorcerer's apprentice. Prodded.

'Look, Miriam,' I said. 'It's wrong that he's told me to keep this to myself.'

'What?'

'This letter and the other things.'

'What other things?'

'A strange photo and a newspaper clipping. They were with the letter.'

It was then, with some kind of sibling telepathy, that Miriam came out with it, allowing me to discuss what I'd needed to: 'Gabriel died.'

'I know. We know.'

'I mean he died young. Two or three? Do you remember the picture of him with Ralph and Vera? He was sitting on Vera's lap.'

'Held there.'

'What?

'Vera had her left hand behind his head. You could see. She needn't have. I mean babies that age can sit up. Can't they?'

'So what about the couple of years before he died? There are no pictures. No-one said anything.'

I told her about the cutting from the *North Devon Gazette* Ralph had sent me. It was No. 26 in its 'Peep Into The Past' feature. The same *Waverley* we were to board the following summer is due and a crowd has gathered in the harbour at Ilfracombe. The photographer has gone for an arty shot, with some of the sightseers close up and the file of day-trippers on the pier in the distance, waiting to embark. With a Biro, Ralph had rough-circled a couple who can be seen a few yards from the photographer and sideways on. From pictures we've seen of them taken at about the same time; they appear to be our father and Aunty Vera. It's doubtful if anyone in the picture knew it was being taken. Ralph had also ringed the date. The photograph he'd sent with the letter looked unrelated. It showed a group of men dwarfed by an elephant, with cameras slung round their necks, in some cases more than one. They were all members of the Coleford Photographic Society on a two-day visit to Bristol Zoo. It was written on the back, with something else. All wearing shorts and floral shirts, they might have been on safari, the elephant their mode of transport. The date of the visit was also noted; Ralph had circled that too. It was the same as the one he'd ringed on the newspaper cutting. Ralph, Vera, and my mother and father had all lived in the Forest of Dean, and were all on that other picture, of the Sunday School expedition. The pre-catastrophe one.

'Well?'

'To be honest, Miriam, it's a bit of a ramble. You'll have to read it yourself. But here's the gist: on the day Ralph went to Bristol with his camera club mates – did you know about that; the club, I mean? – dad was in Ilfracombe with Aunty Vera, waiting for the *Waverley* to come in. The same day. I don't know if mum was aware of it. I'm assuming she was. Probably neither of them knew their photo was being taken by the local paper. And Vera and Ralph must have missed it when it was first published. Maybe they never took the Gazette. As they weren't in the queue for the boat,

I assume dad had got there by other means. Or stayed overnight maybe and caught the next day's sailing.'

'Stayed overnight!'

'Ralph was away for two days. There's a photo of him and his pals with an elephant giving rides.'

'An elephant! What are you talking about? What is he saying?'

I mentioned the zoo and rustled the letter, all three pages of it. To make it sound as if I were checking. But all I could concentrate on was the green oak tree embossed in the top right hand corner with the nursing home's name sprouting from it. Oakland Vale, Barnstaple. I'd tried to read the letter over and over.

'Then he goes on about Gabriel,' I said, 'giving the little 'un's date of birth. Do you remember dad going at all, before we went to see the baby that time?'

'No I don't.'

'Me neither.'

I prepared her for the letter's core, its garbled, often illegible, heart. About having another child, 'a replacement' for Gabriel. Ralph was keen but Vera wasn't. Vera didn't want 'more sadness'. I asked Miriam to guess how long they'd then been married.

'Well, we went to the wedding and we were both little. Four years maybe? You've seen the photos.'

I had. Miriam was fixed on the silver horseshoe and I was trying to tug myself away to chase something out of shot. Kids. Two uncommitted mites among a rank of settled adults about to say 'Cheese'. My aunts and uncles and mum and dad, and lots of others, coupled, paired off.

Miriam used to be more interested in family history than I am. She enjoyed establishing links, making discoveries: that Ralph was our uncle and that the Ralph-Vera branch no longer bore shoots. In that wedding photograph, all are assigned. Even Miriam and I are, and our parents' effort to keep us under control at that wedding is just one of the joys of parenting. Twenty years later, Miriam would be spoken for too. But not me.

'Spoken for' is the term Ralph uses in his letter. Vera was 'spoken for'. As for Vera's wish to avoid 'more sadness', he says, 'I didn't have it in me.'

'So you are putting two and two together,' Miriam said. 'Good grief!'

'You need to read the final paragraph. Actually there are no paragraphs; it's one long screed.'

'What does it say?'

'I'll pop round. We can try to decipher it. There's a drawing.' (There often was in Ralph's letters.)

Miriam lives not far from me. She's divorced. During the marriage, there was violence towards her of all kinds. He 'knocked her about', as the oldies say around here. We guessed only when it was too late, when it became obvious. Now, if she's meeting someone new, a man, I grow apprehensive. When I once warned her about the need to take care, she scolded me in a sisterly way. 'What do you know?' she said. Well, I've never married. So I know nothing. I thought it a shame but inevitable that her question was half-dismissive rather than a plea for help and advice.

We sat at the table, with the three-page letter, the newspaper cutting, and the photo laid out before us, like unexamined maps, or a last, late conundrum from Uncle Ralph. Miriam has a grandfather clock inherited from our paternal grandfather. It always makes us smile: a grandfather's grandfather clock! It ticked quietly in the background with low immemorial thuds.

Seeing our father and Aunty Vera together in that newspaper photo was strange. They were standing close to each other. It was like encountering for the first time an aspect of a person's life one had hitherto not suspected, a contribution to a wider picture, something nonetheless faintly disturbing.

The zoo picture was a black-and-white box camera print: small and square with a wide border and sharply focused. It was comical but the comedy seemed to be at the expense of something deeper, more tragic, more colourful. Written on the back with the other information was a strange legend: KANDULA – BEFORE HE DIED.

The drawing in the middle of the letter amused us. It was of a tadpole with a glum expression, a black eye, a head criss-crossed with sticking-plasters, and a drooping, damaged tail. Typical Uncle Ralph humour.

Ralph's story jumped about a lot and was often indecipherable. But Miriam and I agreed on the following translation.

Vera and Ralph had 'tried' a long time for a baby. Gabriel's arrival surprised them both. But Gabriel was damaged. That's the word Ralph uses in the letter. After Gabriel's death at around two years' old, and despite Vera's not wanting 'more sadness', they 'tried and tried again' for another, but were unsuccessful.

The tadpole drawing was supposed to be a single spermatozoon, or 'sperm', as Ralph calls it. When he was told by doctors that his 'count' was low, he assumed that one single damaged sperm among his slim population had struggled inside Vera and united with her 'gubbins' to conceive Gabriel that time. Afterwards, in their quest for a Gabriel replacement, none could 'make the trip'.

This is where Ralph's tale becomes sinister, and the point is marked by a change in his handwriting, which is almost illegible. Whenever I think about it now, I have a picture of Ralph, no longer the amusing wizard but now sitting in the darkness as a Devon night falls, his face a seething mask and his anger and confusion emitted in quiet animal noises as the other residents of Oakland Vale settle down to receive their evening meals. I see him with the *North Devon Gazette* opened at its Peep Into The Past page and its picture of my father and Aunty Vera standing together with as much intimacy as they can risk in public; and the date – a date engraven on his memory as the one on which he and other members of the Coleford Photographic Society, with several others, saw an elephant collapse and die at Bristol Zoo, the very animal beside which they'd had their photo taken not thirty minutes before. His imagination surges and zig-zags. While he was away from ROSMERGY, Vera and my father – Miriam's father and mine – were together. In their embraces, 'our young Gabriel came about.' (Miriam forced a smile at the use of a nautical expression to describe a tryst at the seaside.). Ralph concludes: 'It was punishment, see; for your Aunty Vera for being a wickd (sic) woman. Wicked. Tell you father that. Tell him. Tell him it weren't my bad sperm.'

Miriam and I cannot tell our father anything. Uncle Ralph, we've discovered, was a lively resident of Oakland Vale; he entertained with card tricks and wore evening dress and a moth-eaten red fez. We wondered if that was still the case, whether we'd been told it before Peep into the Past No. 26 had appeared in the local rag. Maybe Uncle Ralph had entertained there for the last time and that soon for him all would be embittered twilight.

We have kept Ralph's disclosures to ourselves. There seems no point in telling any other member of the family. I think Miriam, still trying to repair her own damage, has completely forgotten them.

But now and then I retrieve that cutting of my father and Aunty Vera and peep into their past. If it is really them. The man definitely looks like my father as he would have been at that age. About Vera I cannot be certain – not as certain as Ralph. I use a magnifying glass to scan the picture, and it settles where my father's hand appears to rest on Vera's arm. As I raise and lower the glass, the dots from which newspaper pictures are formed expand into an abstract pattern of their own and then recede to form part

158

of the image again, as if by magic. But the point at which my father's fingers touch Vera's skin and, more crucial, make an indentation, falls somewhere between the two and is as elusive as one of Ralph's vanishing tricks.

By the way, I Googled Kandula. There was a famous Kandula from Sri Lankan history, but it took me ages to find the small item about the one at Bristol Zoo. It must have been quite a sight, not to say dangerous: an elephant dying on the spot and rolling on to its side, with a thunderous bump and a cloud of dust, its wild eye for a few seconds fixed on a screaming, scattering crowd. I'm surprised there's no other record of the incident. After all, I've been alerted to the date – twice.

# OTHER WORLDS

It's always there in the distance, like an invitation, or a dare, in the clouds. It never moves as a tree moves in a gale. It never wears out or changes shape, as we do who cling to the tree's trunk, blinded by wind and storm. Picking our way up its flanks or dancing on its summit, we make little impression. Our victory is nothing compared with the mysterious triumphs that earn Ingleborough its garlands of autumn mist. It was there before us and it will be there when we are gone. It marks time. One of its small pebbles might roll an inch to the side, unseen; nothing more. Ingleborough suffers no loss.

I didn't write that; it's in a guidebook to this place and its local mountain. I've been written about – lots. When Stephen went missing, people would say they saw it in the paper or on TV. Parents Tell of Son With Heart Of Gold, was one of the headlines.

What the newspapers didn't explain was how Alfie and I had grown apart before Steve disappeared. Those pictures of the two of us looking glum as we stared at Steve's photograph said more than our suffering at his disappearance: they showed two people already drained of feeling and hope at opposite ends of the line. Not even an only son dead – yes, he's dead – at 28 could fully repair what had been broken.

The summit of Ingleborough can be seen from one of the front upstairs windows in a gap between the houses across the road. We have four rooms: the Hutton, the Barbon, the Casterton, and the Cowan. Alfie named them when we took over this place and decided it could do with a few changes. I'd suggested Rydal, Grasmere, Ambleside, and Derwent, but it was a time when I could see things were not quite right between us and I went along with his ideas for the sake of peace. Steve's death threw us together again. It was a collision. There are still plenty of reasons why we shouldn't get on, but now we'll never part. Our future will be about remembering together. We are mended but the cracks still show, never to be opened up again. We walk with a limp, Joe tells well-wishers, without looking at me for confirmation.

The person who wrote that about Ingleborough called it 'a Biblical summit'. I suppose she meant places where people in the Bible went to think or preach – the sermon on the mount; solid ground under your feet; but no-one to bother you. I sometimes wonder what the Winstanleys thought of it. They stayed in the Barbon that time, out of season, two years after Steve was taken from us. I often think of the Winstanleys, Emma and Joe. I still go back to that year in the Visitors Book and read their names and their comments: February 10-13, 2016 / Joe and Emma Winstanley / Frome, Somerset / What a lovely place. You have everything you could need here. Will return.

They never have. I think guests write things like that to let you know they enjoyed their stay, but don't wish to offend by admitting they'll probably not come back. Some do, our 'regulars'. But most don't; they just want to leave as satisfied customers. It was as normal as it could be. We thought normal would be a help.

The Winstanleys hadn't been here two hours on their first afternoon when we heard muffled but raised voices coming from their room. Alfie threw me a glance, then went on with what he was doing. Then we heard a bump, possibly a suitcase falling off the bed. That was Alfie's explanation, and that's what the bump became. There were no more noises or loud voices. Not for the rest of that day at least. Our guests are never perfectly silent during the whole of their stay here. But most of the time they're out.

I don't know how to put this, but a woman can always tell when another woman is troubled. Alfie and I never let on who we are. Strangers, guests, might have remembered us from the newspapers and TV, but wouldn't guess from our surname, Phillips, that we were the Phillipses who lost a son named Steve in the Middle East. Pictures of Steve are not in the public areas of the building. We are a couple who are getting on with things, despite everything.

As the owner of a B&B, you can't afford to pry too much. But some things are not to be avoided. We have a front room, for the use of guests. Most of the time, it's empty, though in Winter with a full house, we light a fire and keep it going, or invite the guests to. These days, the elderly and retired have extended the season, such as it was. We are pretty busy all the year round. Anyway, on the second night of their stay, I noticed Mrs Winstanley in the guest room, reading a book. There was no sound from the Barbon, and I wondered if her husband was unwell and asleep upstairs. I mentioned this to Alfie. No, he said; he'd seen Mr Winstanley go out, had 'caught the back of him' squeezing through the front door. Later, at about a quarter past ten, I was walking into the kitchen when Mrs Winstanley came out of the room, carrying her book, and began making her way upstairs, clutching the banister. Each step of the stairs makes a faint creak, and I heard the creaking stop for a few seconds half way up, and then resume. Alfie and I were turning in ourselves later, when there was some sort of commotion in the street outside – raised voices, at any rate. Unusual. We sleep at the back of the house, downstairs. Seconds after, the front door banged open, rattling the umbrella stand. Alfie opened the bedroom door to see Mr Winstanley clinging to the newel post at the bottom of the stairwell, then straighten himself, take a deep breath, and march smartly upstairs to his room in a military fashion. He looked a mess.

The Winstanleys said little to each other at breakfast, he bending to his plate of full English, and she gazing through the window at the back garden, delicately nibbling a piece of toast. We discovered they'd just moved to Somerset – from where, they didn't say. We talked about the weather, the news (some Royal scandal or other), and holidays abroad, which we hadn't taken for ten years. They seemed ill-matched: she was well-spoken and courteous; he harsh, worse off, and of few words but not unfriendly, with untidy hair and wearing Sellotaped glasses. He was the first to compliment us on the breakfast. Alfie asked me if I noticed Mr Winstanley's hands. No, I said, not particularly. A woman's hands, he said, white as wax and with long nails. Although it was fine, they never went out on their second day. I don't know what they did for food. On the third, they went out together, she smartly-dressed in a camel-hair coat, he in a grubby mac and wearing trainers. Later that afternoon, I was in the Casterton, preparing it for new guests, when through the window I could see Mr Winstanley approaching, alone, on the opposite side of the road. Thirty yards behind was his wife, walking idly and not as though she'd been detained, but evidently with her eyes on him. When Mr Winstanley entered, he shut the door behind him and, mumbling something under his breath, took off his coat and climbed the stairs, making what seemed like an exaggerated effort, audibly puffing and blowing. It was a bit comical. His wife then rang the bell. Alfie answered it. He could see her beyond the dull glass, like someone coming in and out of focus. She apologised, not for her husband but for leaving her set of keys behind. That night they went out together, for a meal, we assumed. It was raining. I popped into the Casterton, stood back from the street light, and looked out. Mr Winstanley had already crossed the road and was beckoning impatiently to his wife. She was holding a headscarf in place, he was bareheaded, the rain already having made a further mess of his hair. When they returned, not late, they seemed to be having an argument, and trying to keep it quiet. I didn't hear it, but Alfie did, turning the TV down so that he could concentrate. Later, there were raised voices from their room, Mrs Winstanley's this time. But not for long.

On the morning of their departure, Mrs Winstanley was first to the breakfast table. We had another couple in and a single man, likely as not a travelling salesman. The couple were hoping to walk the three peaks – Pen-y-ghent, Whernside, and Ingleborough – but as they told me about it I could see that Mrs Winstanley had been crying. How can you tell? Alfie asked me. I just can, I said. As Mr Winstanley entered the room, his wife turned to look at him and her gaze followed him to the table, as a mother's would follow a child. He'd brought a newspaper – the day before's – and read it without exchanging a word. It was one arm of his specs that was taped up. His hair was tangled, his tie carelessly knotted.

On leaving, Mrs Winstanley signed the book, as her husband struggled down the stairs with their two small suitcases. He'd paid us after breakfast. She left first, he awkwardly negotiating the front door behind her. He was wearing the same pair of trainers.

A few days later, Mrs Winstanley sent an email, thanking us again for their stay but trying, I don't know how to put this, to apologise for something. I replied, saying we were glad that she and her husband had enjoyed themselves.

Almost immediately there was another email from her, saying, oh, Mr Winstanley wasn't her husband; he was her brother. It arrived as if flung at the screen from someone who wanted to make contact, not just to explain, especially as the explanation might raise as many questions as were inappropriate to people just pecking at computer keyboards.

They'd asked for twin beds – not unusual with older couples. Alfie thought it was still odd; undressing and all that. I wanted to tell him that he suspected everything but knew nothing, the reason why, before Steve's death, we had grown apart, though I know I must have been a trial for him, one way or another. I stayed silent, of course; I do these days, for the sake of calm.

I wanted to start a conversation, call Mrs Winstanley Emma, and tell her about Steve – how he was an aid worker who'd been kidnapped in northern Syria in 2012 and then beheaded by terrorists two years later.

But I somehow know we won't see them again. They are in another world. We all are, in our own ways. So she'll never find out about him and us and we'll never know about them – unless we read about them in the paper after something awful has happened. Just as I'll never know what's in that video. Alfie forced himself to watch part of it, because it was the last image of his son and he wanted to rage, he said – rage; his son, not ours, he said, though Steve is ours, was ours. I know they block out the final minutes, I know the murderers shout something foreign. But I could never bear to look. Alfie did say the place where it was done was like the top of Ingleborough, with men in black wearing black headdresses that flapped in the wind. I cried at that.

He called me 'old girl' and placed a hand on my shoulder. Then he went out, perhaps to shed a few tears himself. At least, I heard him blow into a Kleenex, perhaps so that I should hear. Well, I did; I did hear. Nothing will change for us now, like nothing changes for a woman with a disturbed brother, or on mountain tops, apart from a pebble dislodged an inch or two by a gale. Nothing really.

# ON BOARD WITH THE TOLLIVERS

'Welcome to the Chatanooga thingumee!' Mo Tolliver hollered, as we entered the compartment. 'We think it may be carrying a full set of its own spare parts.'

'We hope it is,' Jean Tolliver corrected, greeting us with a smile that beamed apology for her husband's lack of politeness. They looked tired and in need of their refreshment, such as it was.

We were on the Budapest-Prague express, and there was no reason to suppose that the Tollivers were anything other than an elderly American couple balancing their exasperation at poor service with acceptance of it as part of a Central European quaintness they'd read about in books. They introduced themselves with a haste we found odd.

'Cold and hungry – isn't that just about the world's worst combination?' Mo asked, his wife agreeing with a nod while looking at us for support.

Helen and I had boarded the train fifty miles short of Prague after visiting Kútna-Hora, where the cathedral was closed and in one place daubed with graffiti. It was a steam train with old-fashioned carriages. The Tollivers were sitting opposite each other in the window seats of an otherwise empty compartment, eating from a huge bag of bread rolls.

It was called an express but its lumbering progress seemed to confirm and deepen the Tollivers' sense of cheery disappointment. It struggled to reach the speeds associated with a lengthy journey by rail and for miles at a time it slowed to a crawl, often through areas of poverty and dereliction, as if the driver or the railway people were making sure we missed nothing of the country's sharp contrasts. It was Mr Tolliver, often with his mouth full of bread, who drew our attention to it through a dirty carriage window. We didn't let on, but we'd already experienced it on the outward journey – abandoned rolling stock frozen by rust, and overloaded carts drawn by thin and tired ponies, their drivers sitting sideways on with whips extended like fishing rods.

The Tollivers had flown to Vienna from London, travelled by train to Hungary, and then, with an urgency for which the reasons were unclear, caught the juggernaut we were now on and settled for a journey without official means of sustenance. In Budapest, Mo had left his seat to buy rolls from a platform vendor, only to see the train begin moving out early; he'd had to run and leap back on while it was slowly accelerating, his wife barely visible behind the window's grime, struggling to open the ventilating quarter-light above her head.

Helen and I were just drifting around Europe after our A-levels. Some things we saw left lingering impressions, covering like a blanket the subsequent ones. That same day, after leaving the train, we'd had to catch a bus to Kútna-Hora. Everyone clutching the chrome handles on the seats in front seemed to be holding the vehicle together as it moved. Across the aisle from us was an old woman with a chicken in a plastic bag. The chicken's head was sticking out and it was panting, its eyes wide as though aware of a grisly fate. Against the threat of showers, the woman herself had covered her head in a scarf improvised from a similar bag to the chicken's. Even as ragged students, Helen and I looked better off than the other passengers. In Wenceslas Square, the day before, Helen had been almost run over by a legless beggar on a skateboard-like contraption which he propelled with a clump of wood in each hand. It was straight out of a 1920s street scene by George Grosz. We knew that from sixth-form Art Appreciation. The graffiti on the sides of the barred cathedral in Kútna-Hora dripped in mid-sentence, the messenger evidently having fled before full delivery.

'Are you guys hungry?' Mo asked. 'You're welcome to a bun but there's no filling, not even a dollop of sauerkraut.'

He was serious but Jean laughed like someone who had been plied with sauerkraut every hour for all the time she had been away.

'He could have bought some from the same fellow but it would have meant being stranded in the middle of nowhere without a dime,' she said.

We declined. We'd bought sauerkraut on our arrival in the Czech Republic. It lay unopened in the fridge back at the Prague flat we were renting.

'Say – do you have any water you could sell us?' Mo asked.

With our bulky backpacks, we must have looked like people who might have had plentiful supplies. We had four small bottles each. They insisted on accepting only one, though we offered them two. Mo guzzled first, before wiping the bottle on his coat sleeve and passing it to his wife. We refused payment, quickly wearing down their persistence. It was odd, but slaking his thirst precipitated a kind of confession from Mo, a liquid thing, trickling to begin with but promising a cataract. It was all a bit scary, unexpected. The train rumbled on, clunking over points.

'We had to come, you see,' he began. 'Necessary journeys. Is your journey really necessary?'

Helen and I exchanged glances but Jean chuckled. 'He's quoting. Remember that wartime thing in your country to save gasoline, that slogan?' she said.

We did vaguely. Mo swept vagueness aside, dredging detail before we were ready for it.

'Mrs Jean Tolliver here, aka Jaffe Goldgruber, had to go back. Didn't you, hon? Not for the usual reason, mind you, the boring, told-a-million-times reason, how the family were rounded up, pitched into trucks, taken to Ricse, Kistarcsa, Sarvar, the Hungarian transit camps before the Great Onward Journey to the killing-fields. Did you know, by Christ, there are people who are saying it never happened. Check that! Never happened, for Chrissake! It must be dumb cold where those characters are.'

Jean leant towards her husband and placed a hand on his knee. I think we expected her to console us, not him, for the monologue that had begun to make our minds grope for connections. She must have been about seventy, he not much older.

'She got out – didn't you, honey? – shimmied up a drainpipe in the waiting room. Waiting room, be bollocked, if you'll forgive the French. Left her best friend behind, little Aliya. Do you know what it means? Aliya – To ascend, go up. You couldn't invent it. Never recovered, did you honey? Tiny Aliya, who was too scared to do what her name told her she must. Then the march to Bergen-Belsen, then you wonderful Brits going in. Jean here – d'you know what Jaffe means? It means beautiful. Beautiful Jean, the survivor.'

Jean turned her head slowly towards us. Was it out of pride, embarrassment or confirmation? Then the compartment door was slid open roughly and a ticket-inspector stood before us with his hand held out. Jean rummaged in her bag. She was shaking. I reached for our tickets and Jean held out theirs. The inspector looked at them, eyed us one by one, and then mumbled something before slamming the door shut. An abandoned railway station slipped by, its windows blocked by rotten tin sheets.

'Who died and made him boss?' Mo asked. 'What a *schmeboygah*! Anyway, that wasn't the point. The point was, beautiful Jean made the mistook of going back to Hungary, land of her fathers, the dough-guzzling duh-ta-duhs.'

At this point, as her husband stared out of the window to reflect on his wife's historic lapse of good sense, Jean attempted to join in, with a slightly imploring tone.

'It was my home, after all,' she said. 'I had to go back...'

'But there was no-one there,' Mo cut in, addressing us, not his mistaken wife. 'Talk about breaking the devil's dishes. Why would there be? They'd all been herded together and taken to the ass-end of space, never to shimmy. Eh, Jean, never to shimmy up a pipe and get the hell out! Christ, I'm tired. You guys tired?'

We shook our heads, not knowing whether this was the right response. Perhaps not being tired was an insult to those who could have been nothing else after a marathon train ride. All this Helen and I discussed afterwards, after the events that took place at the end of the journey. 'Anyway, Mo said. 'What about you?'

We told them as they shared their bread bounty with us. It didn't take long. We were Brits and young and callow, and that was enough. Outside it was almost dusk. We glimpsed flurries of snow. We talked some sixth-form politics. Yitzhak Rabin, the Israeli prime minister, was two weeks dead, shot by a Jewish extremist at a peace rally in Jerusalem. We didn't mention it and neither did they. As our self-revelations tailed off, Mo got his second wind. Jean was dozing, her head at rest against the window, her reflection coming into being as the light outside grew dim and the compartment's naked bulbs staggered on. Mo lowered his voice.

'You see, once the mother-effing Russkies came down the lane in fifty-six, the native Magyars took against the Goldgrubers of the world,' he said. 'Never liked them anyway, if you ask me. And who's asking Mo Tolliver? Or Moritz Thalbauer, German Gentile, if my old man hadn't

173

changed his name, the old *weisenheimer*. Like, the Jews have soaked up too much pity? What about us? the Magyars said. Leave some for us, or let us spit in your face. My old man? He wanted to be an American, start from scratch.'

It was Helen who looked puzzled – or concerned: I still can't pin her down. But she was ahead of me then, cutting a path through this waterfall of recollection.

'And Budapest?' she asked. 'Is it the same? Have they changed?'

Mo slumped back in his seat wearily, like someone whose secret has been stolen, leaving him with no prop. 'Have they Jean?' he asked his wife, who opened her eyes as he spoke. 'Are you a stranger in the old country?'

Jean roused herself. 'Well, it's the gipsies, isn't it?' she said, cryptically. 'They hate them. And here, too.' She stared outside with her nose pressed to the window, as if under the street lights she might see members of the scattering dispossessed at the start of the journeys.

While Helen and I tried to think of something to say in the silence that followed, Jean went back to sleep and Mo joined her. With his head dropping on to his chest and the bag of rolls hanging from his right forefinger, he resembled some innocent villager who had just been shot accidentally, caught in crossfire while returning from the bakery. Only his snoring betrayed the life in him. It was loud and uninhibited and made us giggle. Jean was soon at it too, at a higher pitch but much less noisily. It was the briefest of naps, because within fifteen minutes the train was approaching the outskirts of Prague, and they woke simultaneously with a jolt and with expressions gripped by momentary terror.

'It looks dumb freezing out there,' said Mo presently, prodding his wife to wake her. 'Have you guys far to travel?'

We explained that we were staying on the other side of the city, in one of the old Soviet estates, though we didn't mention the Russian connection. They were in a city-centre apartment, a short taxi ride away.

'Well, thanks for your hospitality,' Jean said. If they hadn't been American, their hearts a-throbbing on their sleeves, it might have sounded like a reprimand for not having contributed much to the exchanges.

Mo stepped on to the platform first, followed by Helen, then by me, the gentlemen helping the ladies disembark. As I took Jean's elbow, she groaned.

Walking past the engine, which stood snug and steaming against the buffers, Mo muttered something about 'the Casey Jones Special' and chuckled. He caught my attention and pointed to an oil-smeared engineer who was tapping the wheels. It was there that we parted, almost without formality. We hadn't even asked them what their plans were, or they ours.

Then, as we looked back at them making for the city exit, we saw Jean fall to the ground. Even by the time we reached them, they were encircled, some people obviously knowing what had happened and tending to Jean, and others, still standing, drawn between lending a hand and moving on. The concourse, to dignify the grubby expanse at the railhead with a name it didn't deserve, was in motion, thronged with rush-hour crowds, mostly manual workers by the look of them. Mo had taken off his jacket and had made a pillow of it for Jean's head. Outside the circle lay Mo's plastic bag and two bread rolls – hard, uneaten escapees. A petrified stray dog had its eye on them. We tried to push our way forward but couldn't make ourselves understood. We shouted Mo's name but our voices were lost in the commotion. We watched as the ambulance arrived and Jean was taken away, our roles as the recently befriended usurped by others, strangers with expertise. At least we stayed; at least we waited. We called Mo's name again as he stepped into the back of the vehicle, and this time he looked round, seeking us out but not acknowledging our wave, perhaps not recognising us at all. And that was the last we saw of them.

We made one more trip to Kútna-Hora. The Church of St. Barbara is one of the grandest and most beautiful in Bohemia. It is not a cathedral, as we first thought, and this time it was open to visitors. A workman, the double of Mo's investigating mechanic at the station, was removing the graffiti. The Church of the Most Holy Trinity is a brisk walk out of town, in the suburb of Sedlec. It has three naves and was enlarged four centuries ago. In 1870, the historian Frantisek Rint re-modelled the charnel house, known as 'the bone chapel', using about 40,000 human skeletons. It was amazing. Not that long before we encountered them, we might have said the Tollivers would have loved it, a couple of Americans on the tourist razzle. So many conditionals now. Even the chandelier is a bony work of art.

# CAMERA OBSCURA

There's a new man at the café at Blaizac. Unlike old Clauzon, the chap he's replaced, he's an immigrant; that's to say, he is new to the district and, by the look of him, new to the country. Joseph, the chicken-farmer, says it's the first time he's seen 'a Moor' this far north, but these things are patently relative for anyone who's moved at leisure between, say, Le Puy and Bourges, or who finds the appearance of a nervous black face among so many white ones noteworthy.

The new man says little. He's efficient in a breathless way, as if his future here depends on the outcome of a prolonged trial at which we regulars might or might not be judge and jury. He lives alone at the back of Luc's café in spartan quarters which connect with a mezzanine surrounded by high walls. From this enclosure drifts the sound of a distant Arabic radio station and the hoarse yapping of a puppy dog.

Mind you, we must seem an odd bunch. Auguste is a veteran of the Algerian war. I wonder whether a man like Auguste Delubac, reticent about his part in history, gains or loses by a refusal to reveal all. At any rate, the lack of embellishment from the only source that can account for it hardens the edge of his inscrutability. The grey, upturned brush of a hairstyle, the tightly-packed features and the scar bisecting his right eye invite speculation. As an immigrant in this country myself and a woman, I have twin barriers to clear before I can link Auguste's reclusive life at St. Marguerite with his earlier exploits and discover more about the puzzling circumstances surrounding the death ten years ago of Mme. Champel, Joseph's bed-ridden wife. We chat about nothing more profound than resistant varieties of maize, uneventful *vin de pays* and the neighbouring hamlet of Boucille, currently being taken over by British families in love with mouldering piles of stone. Although English (with some Welsh blood), I'm not considered part of this cultural occupation, having arrived years ago to discover that a strange woman living alone in these parts simply increases the stock of native eccentricity. The curé has a knack of wrapping contempt in extreme politeness.

Thus, there is an atmosphere of spurious calm, which the new man's unceremonious arrival has served only to heighten. His name is Batou and he's Moroccan. Joseph and Auguste treat him civilly but are not anxious to know more, except that Joseph has asked to sample the spicy food whose smell trails over the wall as we make our way home in the afternoon. Joseph soon turns off towards the loaf-of-bread farrier's cottage which has been in his family for countless generations. He too lives alone. There's a feral orchard, a few goats, and an old yellow Renault jammed into what used to be the smithy's cavern. Mme Champel had suffered what sounded to a perplexed inquest like a baby's cot death. An open verdict was returned. Rumours persist, sometimes surfacing, like the evening wood smoke. Auguste just smiles.

Last weekend, as I was strolling past, Batou was outside his back gate, facing the car park. He called me over. There was a direct route into his single back room through an open door. I followed him in. The pup nipped my ankles with its soft milk teeth. Batou had obviously prepared for a brief visit. Opened on a low table was an album of faded colour photographs. As I peeped at it he saw me and said, '*En vacances – les Anglais, les Americaines, les Allemands.*' He took from his wallet a crude and dog-eared business card and a photo of himself armed with a Polaroid camera. I flicked through the memories of old washed-out encounters and imagined Batou darting out from behind yielding palm-trees in his T-shirt and khaki shorts, squaring up to people who must have thought they were about to be robbed. What remained of these advancing forms were their faces, yet even on them a chemical reaction was creating something uniformly grim and beyond recall. Only then did I realise that these represented failed transactions, unsolicited snapshots, and that for some reason he had kept them. The impression was of a relentless surge of humanity, on the whole disdainful.

News of our meeting spread, as it invariably would around here. The mystery of this can be both satisfying and frightening. There are times when the place seems uninhabited, when not even an imagination stuffed with images of bow-backed farmers inspecting their vines can

179

account for the peculiarly emotive nature of our depopulation. Someone must have seen us, someone stopping briefly in the darkness of a room behind a potted geranium, that symbol of homage to the blistering sun from which all seek shelter and derive nourishment.

For a while I felt that Batou's interest in me was as enigmatic as that of Joseph and Auguste. Having momentarily laid down his defences, he should have been wary of any further interest in him, as it would not have been on his own terms. But instead he seemed to look upon me as a potential conspirator. At times like these, one sex sees the individuals of the other blur into an undifferentiated mass as a prelude to generalisation about the hostility between them, and its effects can be the same as those set up by the arcane machinery of gossip. What save me was the absurd idea that Joseph and Auguste would ever consider Batou's gender to be a more powerful common factor than their obvious differences.

'My sister – she comes on the three o'clock train tomorrow,' Batou whispered to me as I, in my silly English way, began rounding up spent glasses.

'That's nice,' I said. 'Will she be staying long?'

'She is always staying.'

I interpreted this as meaning that his sister was a constant burden to him, and I wondered whether or not he were asking me to sympathise with his plight as a put-upon sibling. Perhaps he'd discovered that among immigrants there was safety in a lack of numbers. Then I understood that it was she who were fleeing – and always to whatever haven he could provide for her in this countryside of unbeaten tracks.

It was a fair old run to the nearest station, at St Ambroix. I supposed that Batou might have arranged a taxi. But, having dipped my toe with impunity, I waded in.

'Don't bother yourself with transport,' I said. 'I'll pick her up.'

He reversed a few feet into shadow. His eyes flared as though they had left an impression of themselves behind. He looked at my feet, trying to make out the place where he probably feared to tread.

'And the baby,' he added, without raising his head. I thought of this as the position which others at a different time and in a different place would have fetched him a clout about the ear for his effrontery. Neither of us moved. We both savoured an immemorial state of conflict, knowing that in reality we had already made an advance, however slight. We could hear Joseph and Auguste mumbling politics outside with a passer-by. It was one of those short-circuit exchanges, with words popping like squibs towards anyone who took them personally. This is not a Left Bank *intellectuelle*: here they grab every issue by the lapels and rough them up a bit. Except when I'm around. Then it's small talk, the diversionary tactic of those confronted by someone looking for a way in.

Batou couldn't get time off to accompany me to the station. With a head full of French pleasantries, I stared at the photo he'd provided and recognised the sister straight away, not that there would have been many Algerian women with a young one disembarking at St Ambroix.

The baby was lashed to her with a shawl. As I approached, the question I'd always wanted to ask Joseph and Auguste begged again: how would you feel being a white man in a place where most were black, where both meek and mighty did their worst towards you and where you looked on every other white person as a walking repository of all you remembered and hoped for yourself?

Although I knew she couldn't believe that I was Batou's messenger, she got into the car. I made all the conversation, such as it was – the usual daft stuff about babies. She could tell I was no expert on motherhood. Mothers, I guessed, talked about the worst of times so as to make the best of times open up in silence like a flower after rain, joy being a private thing. She half-smiled once or twice but looked across at me nervously, as if expecting to find an interrogator behind the veil of relaxed inquiry. Her suitcase bobbed up and down on the back seat; though old and split at the seams, its resilience and battered usefulness dominated, and I imagined it snapping open and releasing all the street sounds lived through by its pale-knuckled wandering spirits.

I dropped my passengers at the back of the café, where Batou was waiting. The sun was going down, gilding everything, but it was still hot. Soon, the village loiterers would emerge into a calmer version of their element, shadows would stretch across the square. In such a place an innocent could believe that a secret was impregnable.

It was the following day before a baby's cry made Joseph and Auguste realise that Batou was not alone. For once, Auguste's measured certainty failed him, though Joseph was sceptical when told that Batou had been reunited with his sister and niece. It's amazing how Auguste's unspoken experiences lend authority to his pronouncements. What looks to Joseph like a blank state soon transforms itself into the dark horse which tramples on his doubts. I think they were annoyed at being contradicted. They must have believed there were procedures to be followed before one undermined the cosy intuitions of men.

But Auguste soon began nodding sagely.

'We created more problems than we solved out there,' he said.

And if Joseph had not been more intent on trying to catch a glimpse of the newcomer through the bedside curtain, beyond which she could be seen rocking the baby to sleep, he might probably have agreed. Batou's sister was certainly a beauty, and Joseph soon took to intensifying his enquiries about the cooking as soon as it redoubled. His route to the woman was through the baby, whose ear he tweaked with his tawny fingers.

For three days the sister helped out as a waitress. She was over-zealous at first but it was Joseph's hand on her behind rather than familiarity with custom which made her slow to our pace. Joseph loved it when I held the baby outside, because then he could go inside and pester its mother.

'They'll be gone soon,' Auguste said to me on one of these occasions. 'They won't be here long.'

If I gazed over his shoulder I could focus on the weathered poster of Le Pen wrapped around the telegraph poles in the square. When Auguste's features re-established themselves, they, too, broke into a grin like the one on the face of the man he said he'd voted for. In the same way that Joseph was bound to the land beyond my reckoning, Auguste pulled rank on me and my pretence at fellowship. I hear tell that he'd once seen an infant sliced clean in two like a watermelon, '*pour encourager les autres*'. But he was right. Within days, mother and child had moved on. Cars, silver specks, whizzed past on the distant main road again; only I had temporarily forgotten them. For Joseph and Auguste they are constant reminders of how many pass them by and ignore or ridicule what they say, or fail to acknowledge their existence at all.

Perhaps the civility of Joseph and August is just French. Pure charm. It's easy to fulfil stereotypes here. What with all those Simenon potboilers and my English friends' yearly confirmation of idyll, you don't know where you are. The track leading to my place from the St Ambroix road will take a car's width but little more, and peters out in a mud-turning-circle further along. If you then take the footpath past Joseph's copse, you can see the English tower, *le tour Anglais*, stoic survivor, maybe by sheer architectural dullness, of the Hundred Years' War. I used to cycle down there but stopped after finding a single unlaced shoe at the circle's edge. It takes about four days for guests to realise that the barking of Alsatians at the junction farm is a hollow threat and sometimes never do they learn that the dogs are permanently tethered to long, heavy chains and for that reason rarely rise on all fours in obedience to their menacing approach of their owner.

So, could it be that we who work our way up through the murk and enjoy the surface only for the light it casts on things slightly submerged will never know the comfort of immunity, that sense of hovering always above what is supposedly real? To confound the instincts; that's the deepest pleasure.

It's something I try to do with Joseph and Auguste, but they are more than commonly stubborn, like most men, especially my late husband, Harold, who got on with them almost as well as he did with me. From our table, we can see the Church of the Assumption where Joseph's wife is buried, and I sometimes think of the circumstances in which the body of frail Marie-Louise Champel, the skullsmile having finally broken through its skin parchment, emits the faintest of shudders, like something falling in on itself, at the appearance of yet another tributary in the alabaster delta above her.

As I scrutinise Joseph and Auguste and wonder whether or not the grains in our coffee cups foretell the penalty to be paid for pleasure, even the pleasure of thinking that an intruder, a stranger, can make no mark on our idea of stability, the intruder himself advances, smelling sweetly, out of the void.

# THE TELLING AND SHOWING
# OF MAXIMILIAN

Max. Which is all there was to him, really. A three-letter name. 'It's short for Maximilian,' he used to say, but he was joking. So we knew something about him: that he wanted us to understand in his clever way that he was 'five-syllable sophisticated'. We also knew that he'd probably got a girl into trouble, as they say around here, and had once been banned from driving after being found drunk at the wheel of his car following an accident. It was a long time ago, pre-breathalyser, and late teen stuff. But he was coming home.

There were six of us waiting: his mother, his sister and brother and their spouses, and me. Drink had been taken, except by the mother, a ninety-year-old lapsed Methodist, her liveliness at last muted. There were silences. And a lot of getting up and walking around. In one of them, imagination played: a car zooming up the valley (he'd long served his disqualification), its headlights full on; and those two – the roar and the full beams – becoming real in the distance as we stiffened to face what we had to face. Max. He'd kept himself to himself.

What we knew of him before he left:

*Prize Day*

'And the English essay award goes to Max Fisher.' Applause. Half-smiles and polite clapping from the staff, a semi-circle of downside-up bats (as he later described them in a magazine interview) who were not to be answered back. Max had thought Yeats over-rated. And said so. Eloquently.

*Incident at Fulgoni's*

We heard it from widower Lemuel, the big Pools winner who lived sadly on his own with a bulldog called Bosun and kept his dead daughter's fur coats in a wardrobe. Max had been thrown out by the waiter Flavio Gazzi, he said, for being abusive, and was screaming at passers-by. Lemuel didn't know Max: some red-headed lout, he reported, who'd been 'at the gut rot' and was taken away by the police.

*In the Matter of the Pudding Club*

It could have been anybody's, they hissed, but Janine knew it was probably Max's. There were no ways of properly telling then, but her cousin Sue's parents in Kircaldy had gone to court, and Sue's story was all over the Fife Free Press for weeks, so she didn't bother. Poor Sue. It turned out that the respondent was not the father. Paternity suit it was called, like something a dad might wear to a christening. Sue named her son Rory. Janine named her daughter Isobel. The bastards.

*Scene at The Goose & Cuckoo*

The landlord was ticked off in court for serving Max drinks when it was obvious he'd fuelled up before arrival. The

187

locals liked Max, the lone nineteen-year-old regular with the Frogeye Sprite some garage-owner friend had let his father have for a song. 'The Rat & Pickled Egg', Max called the place. The tree he drove into is still there, ever waiting for all-comers. He later fictionalised the crash, describing animals which 'came silently out of the night' to investigate the hissing car and its driver, bloodied and asleep against the steering-wheel.

*

The view from here big-dippers down the slope to the valley bottom, where a vein of neon light tracks the way out. Max took it one night when his father was pick-axing below for black gold, and hardly ever returned. It's another world now. Winding gear has wound itself into the ground. Cataracts that were once just stifled drips thunder beneath – so they say. The invisible gas that would ping a canary off its perch like a pock-marked target at Danter's Fair now swirls in abundance. The past down there is a space being refilled.

We could have talked about Max but we didn't. We speculated on why. Someone said it was a long time since his novel, *The Unbridled Guest*, was reviewed in the Sunday papers, though not ones that most people around here bought. Cuttings would be sent by others that mentioned him in passing: at raucous parties in Berlin and the south of France. There was a follow-up to the first book but it was a pebble cast into a fast-flowing brook: it caused no ripples, and got left behind by the glittering onward rush.

Anyway, like Max, we've shuffled towards the abyss, those of us who haven't vanished already before their time. We head the queue. Behind us are the frolics we once enjoyed ourselves; the spent party-poopers and pointed hats, music's dying fall. We are growing old, and the prodigal is coming home.

Max never wrote many letters. When humanity stopped doing it and went digital he more or less gave up communicating altogether. So the last one had come as a surprise. He's not on Facebook or anything else. Being 'on' anything would probably irk him. He had his standards. He used to write to me once every couple of years and I understand his sister received the odd missive. It was all about thoughts of himself. Max's shortcoming was his neglect. No-one had his postal address or his phone number. It was as though he didn't want us to believe he existed any more.

The sun leaves the scene early here. Sometimes, having sought a gap in the hills, it nevertheless illuminates a high cluster of trees, pointing out some Arcadia destined to fade. Now, it has grown dark and cold. Eventide, as our long-forgotten hymns have it, has passed.

His brother reminded us that Max was always on time. And so he was.

We gathered and stood back from the window, with just his mother's table light on. It was an attempt at a surprise by those who had lost faith in surprises. Far from 'roaring' up the hillside, he came quietly, his headlights dipped, and pulled slowly into the yard in front of the house. He seemed to need help in getting out of the car; but he managed it. Dressed in a thick herring-bone overcoat and with his hair grown long and yellowing – ginger turns gold – he looked older than we expected. Half way to the front door – I'd put the outside light on – he stopped and looked up at the stars. He appeared raffish in his corduroy trousers, red shirt and orange-and-blue tie. We didn't go out to greet him; we waited till he knocked. His overcoat seemed an encumbrance.

'I'll go,' I said to the others, as they clustered around his mother like nestlings.

Under the porch light I barely recognised him.

'Maximilian,' I said.

'Jan,' he answered, half-grimacing.

He brushed past me. I could smell drink, cigarettes.

Tea and cakes were brought out and we settled into muted talk of the old days. It was a while, but not that long, before he told us how many months he had left. And only much later, when his mother had gone to bed, the others had departed, and he was smoking without having asked if I minded, did I break the news that Isobel had agreed to seek treatment.

*In the Matter of the Self-Harming*
Just to say that it's been happening for a while now.

'I never knew,' he said, leaning across but meeting some undefined obstacle. 'Poor Izzy.'

There was a lot the all-knowing Max didn't know, but I knew some of it; and, being one of those who'd stayed, I could comfort him with the knowledge he'd discarded and left behind, as he covered his tracks in all innocence. But we could never be an item again – not now (he'd hate the word 'item'). We once had a brief shared history. But it had separated and each was well along its pre-determined path. At the end of his, some evidence of turmoil could already be seen, and some inner wailing, and then silence. At the end of mine? We'll wait and see. But here he was. Back at last.

# EDWARD ELGAR REHEARSES
# THE POWICK ASYLUM STAFF BAND

He decides to walk there, because the weather is promising. In his larger music case, both violin and viola nestle like indivisible siblings (one never knows who might not turn up). He also carries the piece of music to be tried out with them again – this time 'in public', as it were. His father has helped him copy out the parts anew, and the ink is barely dry. In fact, the title of the quadrille *La Brunette* is still smudged, and resembles a hedge ablaze and smoking.

It's a long walk, a healthy one, but his collar and tie are growing tighter. Not to worry: the Powick Asylum Staff Band, with a few talented inmates, has to set an example, so he puts up with it; the green bowler, the buttoned boots, and the tweed three-piece with the watch on a chain likewise. Music as therapy, along with the leafy Powick acres, the pavilions, the cool arbours, the allotment (though for some the concept of a future outcome as they bury the seeds in runnels none too straight is not grasped). All can be dealt with. Only Mr Mordecai Rees, clarinet virtuoso and a patient (Melancholia, with Dementia praecox), currently masquerading as the recipient of intelligence from Mr Ewart William Gladstone, poses a difficulty. Mr Mordecai Rees's twin brothers died in 1854 at, respectively, the Battle of Balaclava and the Battle of Inkermann, and the poor Rees family fell apart. The details are probably apocryphal, but it is rumoured that a Russian cannon ball passed clean through the one twin's midriff, and shrapnel spinning through the air like sparks from a Catherine wheel reduced the other to the appearance of a headless rag doll. Their father being a drunkard, the wretched Mordecai took to the streets and the byways, grubbing and begging for food, and was eventually sent to Powick; the threat of being 'sent to Powick' having long been Worcestershire shorthand, even in the most respectable families, for incarceration among the deranged as a form of punishment. It was Frank Elgar, an oboist, who one afternoon saw Mordecai rocking on his heels before old Frobisher's resting clarinet, as though the acquaintance had been long in the waiting, and Frobisher who offered to teach him. It was not so much tuition as the re-awakening of some inherited but dormant aptitude, for within two years Mordecai (with Gladstone's approval, no doubt) had arrived note-perfect to within twenty bars of the end of Mozart's Clarinet Quintet before exposing himself to the audience, albeit one consisting of members each in a remote world, given to changing their seats every whip-stitch, wandering in and out, and not caring a birch bobbin about the appearance in polite company of a man's dangler. Frank joked that the music appeared to accommodate the outrage rather than suffer outrageous disruption. In any case, there was applause, instigated by a sole-clapping charge nurse on duty in the shadows and with hands as wide as griddles.

He passes through the gates and continues down the drive between an avenue of towering trees. The building swings into view, swaying to his confident tread and curiously silent, its chimneys crawling with gargoyles, those devils protecting the demons within like sentinels appointed by an army of diabolical conquerors. He can see the chairs being arranged higgledy-piggledy on the front lawn. He smiles at the staff's anticipation in deliberately creating disorder because they know that order at Powick is everywhere tainted by the certain prospect of disarray. For a couple of years he has played in the band, his violin part sailing unimpeded through – how shall he put it? – the studied conventionality of the amateurs, an unimprovable thing. Fired always by aspiration and the achievable goal, he knows only its opposite. Has not Mr Samuel Smiles asserted, 'We often discover what will do, by finding out what will not do; and probably he who never made a mistake never made a discovery'? His ship always sails on, through the jetsam of split notes, misreadings, collapsing cane chairs, simmering rivalry, and Powick's cataract of counter-attractions. Among this last – and he can see her at a high window, smoothing her tresses – is La Brunette herself, Miss Molly Smithson of Chaddesley Corbett, who had a baby out of wedlock at the age of fourteen and was 'sent to Powick', as if to prove the old threat meaningful as well as ubiquitous. But Frank, ever the loyal and protective brother, has told him to be careful: Miss Smithson wanders the corridors as an alluring temptress, her modesty barely covered, her nymphomaniac seeking, but never finding,

Mordecai Rees's satyr. This is Powick all over: conditions that have been arrived at now constrained to go no further, their names – Dementia, Melancholia, Nymphomania, Moral Insanity, Satyriasis – giving the place at least the semblance of knowledge fixed and inviolable, and governing the limits of what it can do before assigning a name to an outcome: Recovery, Relief, Inaction, Death. Just those.

The old bandmaster has retired and he has taken over. This is only his third 'public' outing – the Powick band is not bad and its audience captive and undiscerning: visitors, patients, other off-duty staff. As he approaches the entrance and begins climbing the steps, he is humming the *tutti* opening of *La Brunette*, a jaunty six-in-a-bar that propels him skippingly to the front door, where he twirls his moustache. In the distance, emerging on to the lawn, is Mordecai Rees, head bowed and holding a clarinet in his fist as one might hold a bludgeon. What to do about Mordecai Rees? The Powick band is primarily a staff band, its audience Powick's unfortunates and their visitors. Mordecai is demonstrably one of the unfortunates, though with a talent that has risen uncorrupted from the electric chaos of hysteria, and cannot be denied. Frank hopes that Mordecai's loyalties, unlike his realities, will remain undivided. Frank has already arrived.

The Powick Asylum stands monolithic and forbidding, but not on ceremony. That morning there was an interment, the six-hundredth since the place opened in 1848, all tipped into lime pits like burials at sea. Frank tells him that the funeral services in the Asylum chapel are 'an entertainment'. But surely not as amusing as Powick's new Budding 'rotormower', a jangle of parts painted in bright red and green and housed in its own enclosure, an orchestra's kitchen department seeking shelter from a squall. Frank helps out at Powick as well as playing in its staff band – the Elgars, always willing to depart graciously from the norm. In any case, two accomplished outsiders give staff an example to look up to, which made a change from always looking down without much hope of witnessing 'a pearl-fisher suddenly come to the surface who had been thought lost for ever', as one of the physicians put it to him. Sometimes it happens; but only as a prelude to a return to the depths (they watch them swimming back, so falteringly as to suggest the hope of a last-minute return to sanity).

Inside, he heads straight for the anteroom where the musicians meet beforehand to re-construct their instruments, tune them, and trip up and down scales. On the way he is aware of that familiar straggle of wraiths that arabesque around Powick's officious comings and goings. Among them is Molly Smithson, but, heeding Frank's advice, he ignores her; not that she has recognised him. She has her own urgencies to consider at the ends of her fingers, and they do not take in the expectations of a dedicatee. Not that he has inscribed *La Brunette* to her, or that he will, or that she will understand if he does. But that's music: the incorporation in alluring form of all the feelings of the tone-deaf. It was Frank's tongue-in-cheek definition; Frank, who has such high hopes of him, and who

196

is at that moment eyeing Mordecai Rees's arrival at the threshold; Mordecai, beseeching, the clarinet transformed from weapon to offering and held before him in outstretched hands. Not that his previous misdemeanour is now for him anything but an inexplicable blur.

Just this once, is their verdict, and no nonsense. Mordecai nods his head, gratitude overcoming any idea of consequence. Just this once, not ever again. It is like dealing with a child. They are used to that. The fact is that Mordecai is someone they cannot do without. Frank distributes the re-drawn parts. Performances of *La Brunette* are turning out to be easy if rough-cast, even for the Powick Asylum Staff Band. They all play through their music again at the same time in an unintended and cacophonous hymn to the place and its discord. On the lawn, the audience is drifting towards its seats from all corners. Even the Tourettes are there. He once joked to the Superintendent that they could always be heard but not seen, but heard and seen they will be. (There was once a loud rapid-fire SHIT POO SHIT in the slow movement of Schubert's Octet.) The first time *La Brunette* was played, he explained what a quadrille was. Their surly faces turned to him not because he sounded patronising (they needed reminding) but because he insisted on lighting up a cheroot and speeding through his violin part faster than anyone else and without so much as a glance at the music – Edward Elgar, assistant organist to his father at St George's and capable of turning a quadrille into something a quadrille-lover would scarcely recognise; and his name always in the papers. They neither went to the services nor attended his recitals. When they aren't dealing with God's faulty handiwork they are at home wondering whatever made Him reveal it; the mysterious Trinity – you could say that again. Griddlehands is there once more, sparking the applause by example as they stride out of the building in a line to take up their positions.

He leads from the end of their semicircle, his head movements and frequent glances encouraging them to keep up. Someone in the front row – or what passes for a row – gets up after two bars, salutes, turns smartly and marches back into the building. Others arrive in small groups, resembling deaf and blind interlopers chancing upon them in what flashes before him as the supreme example of innocence. A knotted handkerchief on his head, the Superintendent is there, now and then cupping in his hands a bivalve watch but for sure not checking on the accuracy of the metronome markings. There are usually five figures to a quadrille, but he has 'symphonised' *La Brunette*, as Frank terms it, by making each dance express a different emotion. It is not a quadrille for dancing, that's certain; it is for listening to: an invitation to listen to the dance. At its core he has placed a slow movement bordering on stasis that reminds Frank of processional figures on a Greek vase. The band's reception of *La Brunette* up to that point has been mixed. Performing for inmates of the Powick Asylum reminds him of synchronising clocks in a single inertial frame, explained in his new edition of *The World's Encyclopaedia* by Monsieur Poincaré, except that at Powick time is not synchronised, the audience during the opening piece behaving as though the concert has not begun and, a quarter of the way through, suddenly paying attention as though it just has; similarly, at the end, when applause is expected, the audience will still be listening but will need to be shaken out of its reveries by Griddlehands. Anyway, Frank winks at him as the very slow movement, *adagissimo*, begins, Mordecai leading off in measured fashion. It's not long before he notices an undulation in the corner of his right eye, as of white sheets billowing. He sees that Mordecai has noticed it too. Frank and the others are facing the other way, or looking up, transported by his departure, his originality. And he realises it is Molly Smithson, in the guise of Frank's sorceress, swirling about on the fringes of their *al fresco* auditorium, unnoticed, unattended and unconcerned; until she begins moving towards him in the scimitar of greensward between audience and band, like a Muse, not the proverbial source of inspiration but one of the daughters of Mnemosyne, seeking her given authority. Griddlehands steps in, scoops her up under one arm, and carts her off. It jolts the Superintendent but has no effect on the rest of the audience who, he's long discovered, are oblivious to incident except as some undefined and therefore troubling agitation, and in any case are only three pieces into the concert of eight items at the point where the band has two to go. They never know that every appearance of the band before them is a rehearsal for its few public concerts outside Powick's walls.

Afterwards he thanks them for their efforts. They pay grudging respects to La Brunette. He tells them about his

199

forthcoming Bach recital at St George's: silence, apart from wind instruments being de-constructed and snapped with the rest into their cases, and one grovelling inquiry, much stared at. Perhaps their reaction is envy – not of his accomplishments, though that too, but of his ability to come and go freely at Powick. On the walk back, Frank, ever fascinated by what demons control the human mind, talks about Galton's lexical hypothesis of personality, and what remains to be discovered about the brain, about humanity. We are still a mystery, he says; an enigma.

From her high barred window, Molly Smithson, his 'windflower' as he refers to her, watches them pass through the gates, strangers come from nowhere and gone for ever.

# SPECTRES OF INNOCENCE

---

It all began when the suspended garden seat at The Old Rectory in Barrowchurch, Somerset, began gently swaying in the way they do as their languorous sitters get up and walk idly away. For certain, there was no breeze to set it in motion on that windless afternoon; nor were there sitters at all, or any kind of trickery.

But there's a fair amount to relate before we get to that point.

My dad always thought that goodwill, peace, companionship, trust – all the qualities required for the civilised life – were our natural condition. If he'd been a Believer, we might have called him Godly, or God-fearing, insisting on the capital letters. He would have viewed life as a something to be defended against diabolical forces. As a judge on one of our provincial circuits, he had witnessed enough evidence of human frailty and malevolence to have made him conscious of inhabiting a redoubt against the workings of the Devil.

In the courts, he'd enjoyed a reputation for leniency and compassion. Even if religious in the conventional sense, he would have explained the world in his own way, 'rather like the Archbishop of Canterbury', he used to say, in a wry comment on the comical battle between intellect and faith among the highest of ecclesiastics.

We were a family imbued with humanist principles and codes of behaviour that went back beyond my parents' generation. Neither my brother, Michael, nor I disappointed our parents while we were growing up; in fact, I'd heard it said that they were proud of their son and daughter, though my dad instilled in us a suspicion of pride as an unpredicated virtue: the proverbial 'sin', no less, but perhaps not deadly.

Just before we drove to Barrowchurch to view The Old Rectory, Michael phoned me to say he was involved in some kind of financial irregularity at work. The news couldn't have come at a worse time, because our mother had died just three months earlier. We were still grieving. My dad was wretched to the point of being inconsolable; I believe that only the dignity retained from his profession coupled with his own reserves allowed him to remain stable, and he was determined to move out of his city apartment as soon as possible and buy a place in the country. While Michael was explaining his 'spot of bother', I recalled another phone exchange with him twelve years before. He was then a college student and his girlfriend was pregnant. We'd never met. Her parents had taken full control without reference to ours. She'd had an abortion; or was 'secured' one, as Michael put it. I still don't know if we were right to keep the whole business from our parents. I felt then, and still feel, that I had become a reluctant conspirator. My dad, having sat daily before a parade of the casualties of circumstance, would have understood and forgiven, if to forgive had been the proper response – sometimes, he once said, there were no perpetrators in the world, only victims.

Two years separate me and Michael. Our parents were in their late thirties when they had us. My mother was sweet and always in awe of my dad, a reaction he quietly but continually tried to undermine with admissions of his own weaknesses, not with much conviction. In a family like ours, one little troubled by worrying events, there occur what I must describe as 'visitations'. Arriving from nowhere really, Michael's phone calls were examples. He was subsequently charged with minor fraud and pleaded guilty. It couldn't be kept from my parents. My mother never came to terms with the matter, but my dad was sanguine and tacitly forbearing. My mother's breast cancer was another: there was a lump, an urgent consultation, a biopsy, surgery, and then an almost immediate recurrence, before a death, we believe, deliberately hastened by the GP, possibly in league with my dad and the consultant.

As Michael and I drove him to Barrowchurch, about thirty miles from where he lived in Bristol, my dad sat in the back, not saying much but staring pensively out of the window. He'd convinced us, despite our mild reservations, that he was doing the right thing. We'd seen pictures of The Old Rectory, and the village's website – it had an uneventful webcam – presented a picture of tranquillity and modest historical interest. We chatted about this and that. He'd told us about the Carter sisters, the two spinsters who with their clergyman brother, Alfred, had moved into the house in

203

1897. Later on, they were the only ones for miles around to own a car, yet within six months of taking possession of an Austin Windsor saloon – there must have been money in the family – the sisters were dead, their necks broken when they unaccountably drove into a ditch, having left their brother to walk his rounds. Michael, more fanciful than I, had pictured the scene: the car at an angle; the radiator hissing steam; the sisters' felt hats floating in a reen; a shattered windscreen; the sisters themselves, dressed in black and still seated, the black feather collars of their coats fluttering silvery in the wind; their heads lolling impossibly on their chests; but no blood; and no-one around for a long time.

In the discussions with dad about buying The Old Rectory, we'd mentioned these macabre antecedents, knowing that he would dismiss with a chuckle any idea of a shadow hanging over the place because of them. We could already imagine him sitting at a desk and researching the Carters and their appalling tragedy. He hated the anonymity of the good and the elevation of the bad, so the history of a family not particularly renowned for anything except sudden catastrophe would appeal to him. He'd already said as much, and had received a few interesting details from the sisters' great nephew, the present owner. But this hadn't led to any sort of speculation. We must have been about five miles from Barrowchurch when he confessed to something odd.

'Would you two think it ridiculous of me to hope that I'll meet your mother again?'

I was driving and I looked at his reflection in the rear mirror. He seemed vulnerable, leaning forwards like a supplicant. His eyes were moist; they often had been since our mother died, as sorrow rose unbidden. His question sounded as though she were still alive and had perhaps deserted him, and that some occurrence had led him to hope for a surprise reunion. Neither of us answered immediately.

'Do you mean see her?' Michael asked. There was sarcasm in his voice.

I watched dad lean back and gaze out of the window again.

'I don't know what I mean,' he sighed.

Michael glanced at me. It wasn't the sort of thing anyone had heard my dad say in public; or in private for that matter. We still didn't really know why he'd opted to move to the country, or why he had settled on Barrowchurch and its Old Rectory. It wasn't that far away. We assumed he'd thought it through and reasoned it out. It was the way he did things. I guessed he wanted to say again that he missed mother terribly but realised he would be repeating himself. That was typical as well. But he repeated himself anyway:

'I can't believe she's gone. It's the absence, you know, the void – a vacancy, something that had been occupied by someone still here, now somewhere else materially. But no longer materially – if you see what I mean.'

Michael said, 'Spiritually?'

But dad didn't hear and I refused to comment.

Great-nephew Carter was waiting for us. On the two previous occasions, the estate agent had been our guide. It was the final visit before the sale was completed and dad moved in. We hadn't met Carter in person before. We were introduced and he went outside while we took more measurements. He was polite, if distant. From the landing window I saw him on the lawn smoking a cigarette. He seemed fixed to the spot, catatonic, staring at the ground. Suddenly he turned his head to look up at me, as if he had sensed that he was being watched. I stepped back. When I peeped again, he was running inside. I was alarmed, only to realise it had begun to rain.

The house was old but not irretrievably so. There had been more than a nominal amount of conversion and updating. The interior was airy but not particularly light. Here and there were a few remnants of Carter possessions, not yet cleared. As the prospectus had stated, the garden was small, quasi-formal and not labour-intensive; dad was buying what he'd bid for. In a pink see-through plastic bag of bits and bobs was a framed photograph of a tubby clergyman flanked by two women who resembled 1920s flappers: the ill-fated Carters, I assumed. Hearing the living Carter cough downstairs, I knelt and smoothed the plastic against the photo to see it more clearly. I hoped the bin bag didn't mean the picture was being thrown out. Looking at that happy trio, I thought of our ignorance of what awaits us; well, not so much ignorance as the want of any thought of calamity, or one eternally deferred as a likelihood.

I heard Carter climbing the bare wooden stairs one at a time.

'It was just a shower,' he said, standing at the threshold of the room we were in, almost filling it, though only I had noticed the splashes of light rain on the windows we passed. Maybe he was addressing me. 'When you're ready, I'll show you around the garden.'

The outside tour didn't take long. In one corner of the lawn was a sturdy old tree, and from a branch hung that two-seater swing. 'It was put there by my great-uncle,' Carter explained. 'It's in a bit of a state but we've never had the heart to take it down.' He gave it a little push with his foot so that it creaked on its upper hooks, around which the bark had formed a kind of scar tissue. I had this picture of the Rev. Carter, ruddy-cheeked with exertion and sleeves rolled up but still wearing his dog-collar, accomplishing ham-fisted an unfamiliar practical task as the sisters, smiling side by side and heads inclined towards each other, looked on approvingly. There wasn't a lot else to see. A wall separated the garden from a ploughed field. Carter pointed out the ancient burial ground, the barrow, that had given the village half its portmanteau name. It was just about visible a mile off, at anchor and wobbling on a sea of glinting furrows. 'They say there are burials all about here.' He gestured with his right arm, appearing to include the rectory in his catchment. It was not something that had shown up on the solicitor's searches.

Just days after, contracts would be exchanged. When we discovered that Carter would be there to greet us on that last visit before the sale was concluded, we thought nothing of it, though the owner should properly have been out of the frame. All the items to be left, including a shed of garden tools and a lawnmower, had been negotiated. Before departing, Carter collected the plastic bag. For a man who perhaps should have been wishing dad a happy future retirement, he seemed not so much despondent as perplexed, as though there were something he wished to say but couldn't bring himself to speak of it. Lingering in the hallway and wondering if there were anything we'd forgotten to ask, we could see him standing beyond the porch clutching the bag at his side, like a returning prodigal. Only then, as he locked up and we said our farewells, did I think – stupid, really – that he was keeping something from us.

Dad settled in without a hitch; no surprise there. Someone arrived to set up his computer and we established a Skype link. He joined the Barrowchurch Local History Society, which met on the final Thursday of each month. He emailed us to say the vicar was amusingly trying to 'ambush' him, but that the two of them would soon be 'tramping common ground' if not debating theological issues. He'd agreed to address the Barrowchurch & District Parish Council on some of the more colourful cases he he'd been involved in.

Dad had been at the Old Rectory about three months when we learned that police had visited Michael's flat and taken away a computer and a laptop. This time, Michael and I talked face to face.

'What are they going to find?' I asked, not really believing that a mistake had been made.

'I don't know,' he said.

'Is this another financial matter?'

'Not that I'm aware of.'

'Then there's only one other reason, isn't there?'

He had grown pale and shivery. But instead of reaching out to him I touched his red-raw hand and immediately recoiled, recognising that we occupied places inimical to each other. Once again, his was signalling to us – to me and dad – that it had long claimed him. I didn't even consider forgiveness, or redemption; I thought, bizarrely, that his only hope lay in the intercession of the Rev. Alfred Carter. The police took an inordinately long time to make the case against him.

One Monday evening, while waiting for due legal process, as he called it, I Skyped dad. On Skype he leans forward to speak, so that, apart from the wig, he appears as he must have done in court when handing down a sentence or ticking off a cocky barrister. Over his left shoulder is the door to the upstairs office room he's in; it's always open. In the doorway I noticed a figure, a woman, walk fleetingly along the landing to the right as I was facing the screen. That direction leads only to the second spare bedroom. He must have seen my look of surprise, my open-mouthed dumb show.

'What's up?' he asked.

'Oh, nothing. I just thought...'

'You looked as though I'd suddenly changed shape.'

'Do you have a meeting this week?'

'Yes. Thursday. As usual.'

'Not tonight?'

'Good grief, no. Three hours a month is all I can stand of Barrowchurch's local historians. I jest, being now one of their illustrious number.'

As we continued to speak, my eyes were on the doorway. The figure, the woman, made no return journey. I didn't mention it – her. Which was foolish: it might have been an intruder. I rang back, not knowing what I was going to say.

'Hi. Sorry to bother you again. This sounds silly, but I fancied you were not alone just now.'

'Ah – that would be the Carter sisters. Their brother hasn't made an appearance yet. He's always late.'

Silence.

Then he started to laugh: 'For goodness's sake. You worry too much. Go to bed. I'm fine. And all locked up.'

Before falling asleep, I began to speculate. Had dad met another woman? He was still handsome, attractive in looks and intelligence – 'very bright', as they say. If so, he wouldn't have bothered to ask our permission, being secure in personal morality as well as self-sufficiency. Maybe I'd imagined what I saw. That night I dreamt that Michael had been brought before the court to discover that dad was hearing his case and had refused to recognise him or admit their relationship.

Thereafter for a while it was all peace and quiet, except for two disturbing incidents. Maybe 'disturbing' is not the right word.

Dad phoned early one evening to say that Michael had turned up at The Old Rectory unannounced.

'He wanted to know if I could do something about his case; use my influence. I asked him to what end. I knew the answer to that but I wanted him to say it, to say he wanted me, a former judge, to perjure myself. I told him I had no authority in such instances, and that he must submit himself to the jurisdiction of the court and, if he were guilty, to hope for its mercy. Was I wrong?'

He knew the answer to that too. I said nothing.

'I thought he'd see the error of even thinking that I could help. But then he began shouting about how I'd used my influence to expedite your mother's death. In that, he may have been right. But I was never going to admit to it. I made the mistake of saying that at least his mother had not deserved to have her agony prolonged, whereas he... Well, he was here for barely an hour before he stormed out. I haven't heard from him since.'

Nor have I. His mobile phone is always turned off.

A week later, I drove to the Old Rectory myself. It was a still and sunny day. Dad took me to a pub for lunch. Everyone there appeared to know him, and he introduced me. Back at the house, while we were skirting the lawn and chatting, he pointed to the light-green shoots on the leafless bushes. Then his phone rang (the Carters had installed a bell extension outside the porch) and he went inside. As I strolled towards the swing and was five yards away, it began to sway gently back and forth with a barely audible squeak, just as it had when Carter poked it with his foot that time. I walked right up to it and allowed the seat to bump against my thighs, and I stilled its motion by grasping the chains. Nothing else was stirring. I suddenly felt alone, and for a moment I had the strange feeling that dad had vanished for good.

In the end, Michael was given a suspended sentence and placed on the register of sex-offenders.

There was a small item in the local newspaper. I suppose his misdemeanour in these days of unspeakable degradation was minor. But he and dad are still not speaking. I have never mentioned the image I saw on Skype or the garden seat that moved for no reason. If the Skype figure was a woman dad had met and he was keeping the liaison from us, his secrecy has been maintained. The other day, a copy of *Barrowings*, the local history society newsletter arrived, without comment. Inside was an article by dad called 'Barrow and Church: Paganism and Christianity in the Parishes of Somerset.' He is currently researching the Carter family. He told me that the sisters were apparently no better than they ought to have been, whatever that meant. 'Wait and see,' he added. 'But I believe drink may have been frequently taken.'

The last time I visited him, dad seemed as happy at The Old Rectory as he'd ever been. I've begun to feel that, in whatever way, he has found mum again – maybe even 'seen' her, as I had possibly seen her, or her substitute, busying herself outside his office door. I have never again witnessed the swing move like it did that time. Had the ringing phone summoning him inside also rallied whoever had been there, so that when I looked back at the house after stifling the swing's unbidden motion it had become for the few minutes it took him to take the call a refuge against the consequences of pain and suffering?

It would, on that account, be a place where dad could come to some compassionate decision about Michael. It's only a matter of time. And if he does have a lady friend (he'd smile at that expression) and she offers with his endorsement an explanation for the swing's quiet rocking – say, that it was caused by some infinitesimal subsidence from those burials Carter had referred to – then it would only be for me a case of imagination disappointed. All this reads as though I'm weighing every possibility. Well, I am my father's daughter!

Not long ago, I received the following email: 'By the way, you'll love this. I had a letter from a codger here who'd heard I was interested in the Carters. The Rev Alfred was a monster, she said, an absolute monster. I've yet to determine in what this monstrosity consisted. Do we have here the fury of a rejected woman? Watch this space!'

My innocent father would laugh if I mentioned how tempting it is to form a pattern from all the elements that worry me. But I cannot allow reason to sleep. If it did, what monstrous succubus might stir in the fastnesses of The Old Rectory? Maybe it's already too late, and it has already assumed human form.

213

It's just that, when I drove away the last time, at dusk, and turned to look back before pulling out into the lane, I could see that dad had closed the five-bar gate and was leaning on it and waving; but, behind him, in one of The Old Rectory's upper windows, a light went on. I stopped the car and wound the window down. I was certain of what I'd seen.

'What's up with your electrics?' I shouted, pointing to the illuminated window.

He turned to look but seemed unperturbed.

'It's nothing,' he said. 'Nothing.' And he waved me homewards.

In the court-room, he had watched the worst of the world pass before him. Maybe he needed to be on his own now, to make sense of it with companions real, imaginary, and antiquated. He didn't need Michael and, I believe, he didn't need me. All rise, someone would exclaim when he entered in his wig and robes. And they did. Without fail.

Cockatrice Books
Y diawl a'm llaw chwith

The cockatrice is hatched from a cockerel's egg, and resembles a dragon the size and shape of a cockerel. The English word is derived from the Latin *calcatrix*, but in Welsh it is called *ceiliog neidr*: 'adder-cock.' Its touch, breath and glance are lethal.

There is a saying in Welsh, *Y ddraig goch ddyry cychwyn,* which means, 'The red dragon leads the way.' The cockatrice spits at your beery patriotism.

www.cockatrice-books.com

ANY KIND OF BROKEN MAN: COLLECTED STORIES
ROGER GRANELLI
with a foreword by Phil Rickman

A veteran of the war with Japan confronts the Japanese factory which has revivified his valley. An ageing Navajo on the edge of the desert meets his doctor son's white bride. A young jazz musician walks into a club with a pistol in his pocket, and a young criminal from the valleys who is suspected of murder finds peace of mind on a Scottish beach.

Grounded in the post-industrial communities of Wales, yet encompassing Spain, Malaysia and the Florida Keys, this collection spans the career of a prominent novelist from the early 1990s to the present day. Drug dealers, labourers, invalids and war criminals confront the start of a new century, the death of old certainties and old ways of life, the comforting weight of bitterness and the fearful beginnings beginnings of hope.

'Roger Granelli's books are incredibly hard to put down.'

*The Big Issue*

'His characters breathe, make you care. One day the people that count will realise that Roger Granelli is... the best un-sung novelist in Wales.'

Phil Rickman

OF THE NINTH VERSE
A. L. REYNOLDS

Anwen and her younger brother, Idwal, are inseparable almost from birth. The childhood they share involves harvesting the hay and looking after the newborn lambs in the Conwy valley, though Anwen sees before her the promise of a degree in Edinburgh or Durham and a career as a mathematician, while Idwal seems destined by his strength and skill to take over the running of the family farm. Then, as Idwal's and Anwen's feelings for each other grow darker and more complex, she finds herself put to a terrifying choice.

With a luminous prose that reflects the richness of the Conwy Valley, A. L. Reynold's novel explores both the violent, destructive force of passion and the fragility of the human heart.

*Of the Ninth Verse* has a profound and rooted authenticity that convinces and enchants – an enthralling novel by a writer at the peak of her powers.'

Jim Perrin

a subtly-written, compelling narrative of forbidden yet irresistible love.

Angela Topping

SEASIDE TOWNS

A. L. REYNOLDS

For Anatoliy Yetvushenko, émigré and physicist, it should be the perfect holiday. Llandudno calls to his mind the Black Sea holidays of his childhood in Ukraine, while his companion, Francis, is just beginning to awaken to the possibilities of male sexual love in the first years following its legalisation. But Anatoliy has memories of an earlier holiday in Lyme Regis in the 1950s, where his previous lover, who now lives near Llandudno, left him to make a loveless marriage. With its awareness of the landscape of the north coast of Wales, of quantum physics and of deep time, this novel reflects the search for intimacy and fulfilment in the shadow of political tyranny and sexual persecution.

A chronicler of the region's disappearing heritage

*North Wales Chronicle*

PUGNACIOUS LITTLE TROLLS
ROB MIMPRISS

In his first three short-story collections, Rob Mimpriss painstakingly mapped the unregarded lives of Welsh small-town and country-dwellers. In Pugnacious Little Trolls, he combines the skill and quiet eloquence of his earlier work with confident experimentation, with stories set among the bird-bodied harpies of Central America, among the dog-headed Cynocephali of Central Asia, among humanity's remote descendants at the very end of the universe, and in the muddle of slag-heaps and job centres that H. G. Wells's Country of the Blind has become. In the three stories at the heart of the collection is Tanwen, idealistic and timid, embarking on her adult life in the shadow of global warming and English nationalism.

Where is the Welsh short story going? Wherever Rob Mimpriss takes it.

John O'Donoghue

bathed in white fire in every sense... Borges would happily own them.

Gee Williams

freely and fiercely inventive short stories... supercharged with ideas

Jon Gower, *Nation Cymru*

THE SLEEPING BARD
ELLIS WYNNE
with an introduction by Rob Mimpriss

Three nightmare visions of the world, of death and of hell.

The anonymous poet is dragged from sleep by the fairies of Welsh myth, and rescued by an angel is taken to see the City of Doom, whose citizens vie for the favour of Belial's three beautiful daughters; to the realm of King Death, the rebellious vassal of Lucifer; and finally to Hell itself, where Lucifer debates with his demons which sin shall rule Great Britain.

First published in 1703, this classic of religious allegory and Welsh prose combines all the blunt urgency of John Bunyan with the vivid social satire of Dryden and Pope, and is published in the T. Gwynn Jones translation of 1940, with an introduction by Rob Mimpriss reflecting on its political significance as the union of England and Scotland comes to an end.